NANCY WARREN

BOBBLES AND BROOMSTICKS

VAMPIRE KNITTING CLUB
BOOK EIGHT

ISBN: ebook 978-1-928145-64-6

ISBN: print 978-1-928145-63-9

Cover Design by Lou Harper of Cover Affair

INTRODUCTION

Who invited Death to the wedding?

When an ancient beam falls on one of the guests at Charlie and Alice's wedding, it looks like the work of the deathwatch beetle, an insect that eats old timbers. But fledgling witch Lucy and the vampire knitting club aren't so sure. Could there be a murderer casting blame on the wood-chomping insects?

Meanwhile, the old broom that's always stood in the corner of Cardinal Woolsey's knitting and yarn shop is getting called into service. And not for sweeping the floors!

Between learning a new knitting stitch and flying lessons, Lucy hasn't got time to solve a murder—until it turns out the next victim is someone she loves.

Join Lucy and her eccentric band of amateur sleuths in Oxford as they attempt to unravel a twisted skein of clues and catch a killer without dropping a stitch.

∾

You can get Rafe's origin story for free when you join Nancy's no-spam newsletter at **nancywarren.net.**

BOBBLES AND BROOMSTICKS

*M*oreton-under-Wychwood wasn't a famous town in England. You wouldn't find it on any TripAdvisor top ten list or featured in newspapers, magazines or travel blogs, so it rarely enticed tourists. However, it was a very pretty little village in Oxfordshire with a beautiful and well-kept village green; picturesque stone cottages, some with thatched roofs; and overlooking all, like a tired old sentry, the church tower.

St. John the Divine was originally Norman, built around 1200, according to local historians. Over time it had been patched up, propped up and bits of it rebuilt, but its heart was ancient. Walking in on a warm September day, I felt the sudden chill as the stone walls surrounded me. I thought of coffins and stone mausoleums, which made me shiver, thankful for the blue hand-knit cardigan my undead grand-mother had made for me. I wore it over a blue and white linen dress and sandals.

Soon my momentary chill was dispelled as three giggling women entered behind me. First came Alice Robinson, who worked at Frogg's Books across the road from Cardinal Woolsey's, my wool and knitting shop in Oxford. An excellent knitter, Alice sometimes taught knitting classes for me. Now she was marrying Charlie Wright, the owner of Frogg's Books. I was to be a bridesmaid at their upcoming wedding. She and Charlie were getting married in this church, and we were here to plan the decorations. Flower arrangements for the front of the church and pew bows were both allowed.

With Alice was my cousin, Violet, who was a witch like me as well as a bridesmaid, and Alice's friend from school, Beatrice.

As soon as we entered, there was a table display of information about the church, a brochure explaining its history and a stack of printed sheets that immediately caught my eye.

Deathwatch Beetle

You may have noticed the scaffolding in church. This is to allow us to make a thorough inspection of the roof. As is common in many old churches, St. John the Divine shows evidence of the deathwatch beetle, as discovered by a Timber Specialist. The deathwatch beetle can leave timbers hollow and much weakened. We are currently fundraising to pay for repairs to the roof.

(Donations can be put in the box to the left of the door in the wall)

I looked around and noticed an area on the right-hand side of the apse; I thought it was called—the front of the church. There was the pulpit and, behind it, beautiful woodwork, no doubt riddled with deathwatch beetles, and rising up, the pipes of the organ. At the right-hand side, draped in blue sheeting that barely hid it, was a section of scaffolding. It would be fairly close to where the bride and groom would stand to be married. Did Alice know about this? Would the scaffolding affect the visuals?

I barely had time to wonder about these things when the bride came in behind me. She looked over my shoulder at what I was reading but didn't seem very surprised. "It's very sad, isn't it?" She glanced straight over to the section of scaffolding. "Do you know how the beetle got its name?"

"No." And I was fascinated that she did. Alice not only spent a lot of time reading, but she seemed to collect the most extraordinary bits of trivia.

"The adult males make a tapping or clicking sound to attract mates. The noise is said to foretell a death."

I glanced up at the wooden beams above us and felt my scalp itch at the thought of thousands of lovesick beetles burrowing holes in the ancient timbers above our heads. "So you don't mind about the scaffolding?"

She walked forward into the church. "Well, it's off to the side, and we aren't allowed to take photographs during the ceremony, so I don't think it matters much. Do you?"

I hastened to assure her that I thought the church was beautiful. I did, too. There was stained glass in the gothic, arched windows and medieval tiles on the floor in places, as well as stone memorial slabs. The dark timbers looked ancient and sturdy within the vaulted roof.

"Wait until you see the flowers, Lucy. They'll make all the difference. No one will notice a bit of scaffolding," Beatrice assured me.

Beatrice had an art degree and ideas about how the flowers should be arranged. Alice was happy to let her make the decorating decisions, which left me free to wander around the church. I slipped a ten-pound note into the donation box. It was my favorite banknote, as it featured Jane Austen. Then I walked about trying to make out the names of people memorialized in stone on the church floor. However, time and footsteps had all but obliterated their names. The pews were wooden and featured needlepointed cushions, faded with time, for the faithful to sit on.

I wandered around, my sandals scraping on the flagstones, peering at the stone font, the tattered war banners, the memorials set into the wall that were easier to read, as no one had stepped on them.

Here was one to Henry Herbert, landowner, and his wife, Ann, who both died in 1678. Next to that was a stone with a script that I couldn't read.

I moved on to the next one and felt the ground beneath me shift. Constance Crosyer, 1538 to 1608, beloved wife of Sir Rafe Crosyer, 1528 to 1610. My heart began to thump, and my breath came in quick gasps.

I knew Rafe Crosyer, now, in present time, and even though he was undead and had been for half a millennium, it was still a shock to see his wife's memorial. I knew, intellectually, that he'd been truly alive a very long time ago, but I'd become so used to having him in my life that I tended to ignore his history. It was just easier that way. Now? Seeing this evidence of a past love, carved in stone—well, it was a shock. A big one.

I also tried to ignore my feelings for him, as they were so confused. I suspected he'd be the love of my life if he weren't a vampire. But he was. And while I was a witch, I was still mortal. Every couple has problems, but those were a couple of stumpers.

"Lucy?" It was Violet, and she sounded as though she were far away. "Lucy. Alice has been calling you."

I breathed deep and schooled my face to calmness before turning. *Beloved wife of Rafe Crosyer.* What was wrong with me? In all these centuries, of course Rafe had been married. Probably many times. *Beloved.* Would he one day use that word about me?

I walked back to where the three women stood now in front of the altar. Violet stepped away from the others and intercepted me. "Lucy, what is it?"

I shook my head. "Nothing." And when she continued to bar my way, looking concerned, I added, "I'll tell you later."

"Be sure you do." Because she'd been a practicing witch for a lot longer than I had, she tended to be bossy, even about things that were nothing to do with witchcraft. However, she was the closest thing I had to a sister, and so I sort of liked her interfering concern. We turned together and joined the others up near the pulpit.

"This is where we'll stand," Alice explained. Then she put a hand to her heart. Her cheeks were glowing with happiness. "I can't believe I'm marrying Charlie. Finally."

We already knew the order of bridesmaids. First me, then Vi, and then Beatrice, who was maid of honor. Alice was normally a sensible, practical woman, but today she seemed filled with romance and whimsy. She glanced at us, her eyes dancing. "Shall we practice the walk up the aisle?"

"But there's a proper rehearsal tomorrow," I reminded her. I wanted to get out of this place where Constance would always be beloved and where Rafe had once pretended to be dead.

"Don't be a killjoy, Lucy," Violet chided me. I looked at the three happy faces, as eager as little girls to play brides and bridesmaids.

"Fine, of course," I said.

"Thank you. I feel so sure I'll trip over one of the flagstones," Alice admitted. "I want to keep practicing."

"You'll be fine," Violet said. I saw her lips move and knew she was casting a spell, making sure Alice's path was smooth as she walked up the aisle.

We all walked down the aisle to where the old oak doors would let us in on the happy day. We took our places and Beatrice, who turned out to be a singer as well as an artist, began to sing, "Here comes the bride."

She had a beautiful voice, but we still giggled as we shuffled into position.

"Lucy, go," Violet ordered, "and remember to smile," as though she were the wedding planner. Still, I did as I was told. I pictured all the people in the pews and walked slowly up the aisle in time to the singing. I held an imaginary bouquet in front of me. When I reached the altar, I stopped and turned. Violet was already on the move. She also held an imaginary bouquet, and she smiled as though a photographer was going to capture the moment for the front page of a bridal magazine.

As she grew closer, I heard a sound above, like a creaking door. I looked up, but all I saw was thick wooden beams stretching across and above, supporting the stone roof. When she reached me, I said, "Did you hear that?"

"What? Lucy, you're as nervous as a mouse in a cattery."

"You didn't hear a creaking noise?"

"No. I heard Beatrice singing. You never should have read that information sheet. It's made you imagine things. Pull yourself together." But I hadn't heard clicking or tapping. What I'd heard was more like a groan.

Before Beatrice reached us, walking up the aisle while still singing, I whispered, "On the wall over there is a memorial stone to Rafe's wife, Constance, and it mentioned Sir Rafe Crosyer's date of death, 1610."

She nodded, not looking shocked or even surprised. "What choice did he have? He couldn't stay here forever, not aging. Besides, he'd met Constance here, in Oxford. It was too full of memories so he left these parts. He was gone a very long time. Long enough that no one would ever connect this Rafe Crosyer with the one who lived here centuries ago."

"He must have loved her very much."

Vi leaned in closer. "She was one of us."

"You mean?"

"Yes, Lucy. Rafe's first wife, Constance Crosyer, was a witch."

Alice walked up the aisle, looking thrilled and embarrassed at the same time. Her dark hair was pulled back, but a few little curls had escaped and clung to her cheeks. Behind her glasses, her eyes glowed with happiness.

Then they opened wide, and she stopped in the middle of the aisle as a man's voice said, "I thought I heard singing. What a lovely voice you have."

Naturally, that immediately stifled Beatrice's song. In the silence, we watched a man wearing a suit with a clerical collar walk forward. Alice unfroze and dropped her imaginary bouquet. "I hope you don't mind. We wanted to get an idea of how many pew bows to order." Then, obviously realizing that didn't explain the singing and her walking up the aisle, confessed, "And I wanted to practice walking up the aisle."

"Of course, Alice. Take as long as you like, so long as you're out before evensong."

He joined her, and they both walked the short distance to where we bridesmaids were standing. "Reverend Philip Wallington, these are my bridesmaids." And she introduced all of us. The vicar shook our hands one by one and said, "Please, call me Philip. I'll be marrying Alice and Charlie, so you'll get to know me quite well at the rehearsal tomorrow."

Philip Wallington was younger than my idea of an English village vicar. I put him at mid-thirties, with a high forehead and brown hair that he'd combed back off his face. He had a pleasant smile, with slightly crooked teeth and a serene expression. I felt calmer just being around him.

"Sorry about the scaffolding," he said, motioning to the shrouded metal skeleton. "It will be even worse when we do the repairs, of course. But for now, at least, it's not too unsightly."

"Are you sure it's safe?" I had to ask.

"Oh, yes. We've had a structural engineer look at it. Still, some of the beams will need to be replaced and the infestation treated."

As though belying his words, the beam above me made that noise again.

I glanced up. Maybe Constance was the one groaning, warning me to stay away from her husband.

CHAPTER 2

"*L*ucy, Violet, you promise you're not going to humiliate me?" Alice asked, a worried frown slightly marring her bridal happiness. "I never should have agreed to a hen party. The only ones I've ever been to have ended in vomiting and hangovers." She looked queasy at the thought. "And somehow, I always ended up cleaning the mess."

We both reassured her that we had nothing dreadful in mind. Violet said, "But what kind of a wedding would it be if you had no hen party? I'm not sure the marriage would be legal."

The three of us had agreed to meet at my flat above Cardinal Woolsey's wool and knitting shop an hour before the hen night dinner. We did each other's hair and giggled and gossiped. Nyx, my black cat familiar, grew so fed up with us that she very ostentatiously went to the window and meowed to be let out.

"Honestly, we want you to have a fun time and happy memories of your hen night," I assured her. It was true, we did. On the wild and crazy scale, Alice would score about a .05, so we'd planned an evening that included dinner with a group of women who either lived locally or had come in early for the wedding. We'd also added a few visits to Oxford's famous pubs, because even a woman whose idea of excitement was a brand new novel deserved a bit of fun with the girls before her wedding.

Alice gave a grudging smile. "All right. I trust you."

In fact, there had been some argument among we three bridesmaids about how Alice's hen party would work. Beatrice was all for hitting every pub in Oxford and having all the hens end up in a hotel suite for a massive drunken sleepover. I knew that Alice would hate that, but on the other hand, if Beatrice and some of the other women wanted to carry on partying, who were we to stop them? We compromised by agreeing to start with a nice dinner and then we'd hit the pubs. Alice had to promise to go to the first one. After that, she was free to go home, and anyone who wanted to keep the party going could do so.

Since Violet knew more about English bridal customs than I did, I left it to her to choose the restaurant. She said, "The biggest problem is everybody eats different things. You've got the girls who are on diets and will have a meltdown if you push so much as a lettuce leaf at them, and then the ones who are lactose intolerant, vegetarian, vegan, allergic to garlic, fish, cheese, meat, snails, you name it." She sighed. "Then there are those of us who quite like to eat a proper dinner."

She was right. "What do you suggest?"

"Tapas."

That sounded like a good idea. She managed to find a

small tapas bar with a private room and an extensive menu. That would be our first port of call and where all the hens would meet up. There were fourteen of us, including the bride.

Our next argument had been about what Alice would be forced to wear. Beatrice was all for a plastic ball and chain, a garish plastic tiara, a veil, and a large pink sash that said Bride, matching sashes for us that said Bridesmaid, and sashes that read Still on the Market for all the single girls. I shuddered at the very notion, and I knew Alice would.

I argued against any ornamentation. Violet was somewhere in the middle. When I explained the dilemma to Gran and Sylvia at the most recent vampire knitting club meeting, Sylvia said she had just the thing. Sure enough, next evening, she brought me a lovely tiara, something that a lesser royal might wear. She wanted to lend it to Alice for her hen party. I looked at her with suspicion. "This isn't real, is it?"

Sylvia was very old, very rich and loved jewelry. I wouldn't put it past her to send us out with a headpiece once worn by Catherine the Great. She smiled at me, clearly reading my thoughts. "No. This one's made with crystals. I keep my good tiara in the safe."

Of course she did.

Sylvia also had a solution to the satin Miss America-style sashes that I knew would horrify Alice. "We'll knit you all pretty cardigans to wear. They'll be special but not vulgar." Alice was an excellent knitter, and I knew she'd approve, especially as Sylvia was designing the cardigans herself. And so the vampire knitting club got busy. Always happy to have projects to fill the long night hours and knitting at such speed it looked like a blur to the naked, human eye, they turned out knitwear at an astonishing rate.

I ordered in plenty of wool in the exact shade of the bridesmaid dresses, a soft pink. Alice's sweater was the prettiest and said Bride in white letters on the back of the sweater and then underneath it, Alice and Charlie and the date of the wedding.

Sylvia said they'd fancy the sweater up with beautifully crocheted rosettes on the front and buttons shaped like tiny brides and grooms. The rest of us had the same sweater, without the rosettes or the word Bride. Just Alice and Charlie and the date of the wedding.

I was thrilled. It seemed to me that we'd exactly found the compromise between humiliating Alice with a garish display and still having the fun of dressing up and going out to celebrate her wedding. I hoped she agreed.

Violet and Alice had grown so precious to me in the time I lived here that I was thrilled to be a part of the ceremony. I was excited about this evening, my first British hen party.

I opened the bottle of champagne I'd bought at Marks & Spencer's and poured us all a glass. I was going to make a toast when Alice put up her hand. "Bride's prerogative. Everyone will be making speeches about Charlie and me, but while it's just us girls, may I make one?"

"Of course," I said.

She gathered her thoughts for a moment and then raised her glass. "I've never made friends easily. I've always been rather shy. When I first began working at Frogg's Books, I fell in love with Charlie on the first day. Of course, he never noticed me. And we'd probably have gone on like that for years and years until he married someone else, if it hadn't been for you two."

Violet and I exchanged a glance. We never talked about it, but Alice had been so desperate to have Charlie fall in love with her that when Violet said she had a friend who was a witch and could make a love potion, she'd agreed. The trouble was that Violet thought I needed more practice in our craft and had insisted I help make the love potion, under the direction of a very powerful witch and the head of our coven, Margaret Twigg. The whole thing had gone dreadfully wrong. Fortunately, everything worked out in the end, and Charlie and Alice had fallen in love as they were meant to. Still, if anyone ever asked me to brew a love potion again, I would run screaming in the other direction.

"I wouldn't be here today without the two of you. You gave me the courage to believe I deserved a man like Charlie, and you've been my greatest support throughout my engagement." She raised her glass even higher. "To the two best bridesmaids a girl could have." And then her forehead creased again. "Of course, Beatrice has been my friend for most of my life, and I love her like a sister. There's just something special about you two."

I'd invited Beatrice, but she had an appointment for a facial so she was meeting us at the restaurant.

We sipped our champagne, and then I brought out the sweaters that Gran and Sylvia had organized. Dr. Christopher Weaver had made Alice's. Of all the vampires, he was perhaps the most artistic and flamboyant in his woolen creations, and her cardigan was truly gorgeous. Where other brides might preserve their wedding dresses for posterity, I hoped she'd keep that sweater always. It was a work of art.

I'd wrapped all of the sweaters in pink tissue and put them into gift bags. I passed Alice hers first, hoping very much she wouldn't be too embarrassed to wear the sweater. The vampires had gone to a great deal of trouble.

But when she saw it, her obvious hesitation disappeared. She squealed and jumped up, immediately slipping the cardigan on over her flowered dress. The dress was imprinted with old-fashioned roses and green stems. The sweater could have been made to go with it. She twirled around the room, laughing. "I can't believe it. It's so beautiful. Thank you for not making me wear one of those awful Bride sashes that light up." She inspected herself in the mirror, then she looked at me wickedly. "And I know you didn't make it, Lucy."

We all laughed. It was no secret in this room that I wasn't much of a knitter. Violet and I had discussed it and decided that Violet would have to take the credit for this sweater. "But," she protested, "no one will believe I knitted a dozen sweaters all by myself in a couple of weeks."

"No." I paced up and down and then came up with a solution. "We'll say we found a place online. They exist, you know. You can hire people to knit things for you."

I gave Violet her sweater and I slipped on my own. Alice looked out the window as though her gaze were drawn to Frogg's Books across the street. "That's odd."

Naturally, Violet and I both walked up beside her to stare out the window. A well-dressed couple was just heading into the bookshop holding a large, gift-wrapped package. The silver paper and bow gave it away as a wedding gift.

"What's odd about it?" I asked.

"The address on the wedding invitations is my home. All

the gifts have been going there. Who would bring a gift to Frogg's Books?"

"I don't know," Violet said.

"I don't recognize that couple, either. Of course, Charlie has friends and relatives I haven't met yet." She put on a bright smile. "Do you mind if I pop over and meet them? I hate the idea of strangers at my wedding." She blushed. "Besides, I want to show Charlie the sweater. You two come along, and then we'll go straight to the restaurant."

And so the three of us headed across the street in our matching bridal sweaters. We walked into the bookshop to find Charlie in the arms of the woman. She was wrapped tightly around him, her arms twined around his neck, while her male partner looked on, rather foolishly holding the gift.

Over the woman's shoulder, Charlie looked red-faced and embarrassed. His expression filled with relief when he saw us. "Good. Alice." He put his hands on the woman's shoulders and pushed her away. She seemed to go with reluctance. "Sophie, I'd like you to meet my bride-to-be. Alice Robinson, Sophie Wynter and her brother, Boris Wynter. Boris and I were at school together."

Something about Sophie Wynter reminded me of an icicle. Partly it was her white-blond hair, and she was so thin, her edges seemed sharp. She had large, deep blue eyes set in a pale, narrow face. Her brother, Boris, was tall and strapping. He shared the pale blond hair and the big blue eyes, but while she seemed all wisps and angles, he was as solid as a brick wall.

Alice stepped forward. "I'm so pleased to meet you," she said, holding out her hand. She shook hands with first Sophie and then Boris. He held on to her hand. "I was delighted when I heard Charlie was getting married. Oh, but he was a lad. I could tell you some stories about our Oxford days."

Charlie put on a false chuckle. "But I beg you won't."

Boris guffawed. "No, no. Your secrets are safe with me." Then he winked broadly at Alice. "But I'm open to a bribe."

"Really, Boris," Sophie said in a cold, irritated tone. "No one thinks you're funny." Her cool gaze swept over the three of us. "Have you three been volunteering at the hospital or something?"

We looked at each other in puzzlement, and then Violet laughed. "Oh, you mean the matching sweaters. They're for the hen party tonight."

Alice hastily said, "These are my bridesmaids. Lucy and Violet."

Violet and I both knew the guest list for tonight's hen party by heart. There was no Sophie Wynter on it. "We didn't realize you'd be in Oxford already, Sophie. Please, you must come to the hen party. We're meeting for dinner in an hour." I gave her the name of the tapas restaurant.

I thought she was going to refuse, but Boris said, "Splendid idea. You head out with the girls, Soph. I'll keep the old man company for his last days of freedom."

Charlie did not appear thrilled at the thought of spending the evening with Boris. "Actually, I was hoping to catch up on some work tonight. I'd like to get ahead before going on holiday."

But Boris was having none of it. "Nonsense. Business can wait. I'll make a few calls. We'll get some of the old crowd together." He laughed heartily. "May run into you girls painting the town red."

Sophie sighed as though the whole evening out was a great imposition. "Well, if I'm to go to a hen party, I must change. We'll go to the hotel at once, Boris."

She ushered the three of us toward the door as though she were a farmer and we were three pink-clad chickens. Alice sent a last glance back toward Charlie. I felt that she wanted to stay and speak to him, but Sophie was very commanding, pushing us all out the front door so that we were standing on the sidewalk on Harrington Street before we knew it.

"Well," Violet said, "we should head to the restaurant and make sure we're the first to arrive." Luckily the tapas restaurant was within easy walking distance from Harrington Street. Everyone who wasn't close enough to walk was either staying with a friend or, like Boris and Sophie, had booked a hotel in town. There would be no driving this evening. Violet would stay with me, and Beatrice had invited Alice to stay in her hotel room. I had a feeling they were looking forward to gossiping and catching up.

Boris and Sophie headed off to change and we three continued to the restaurant.

We arrived at the tapas bar fifteen minutes before the guests were expected. Beatrice was already there, finishing up the decorations. Alice laughed and clapped her hands when she saw big pink balloons and the banner that read, "Congratulations, Alice." Each of the three of us carried a large carrier bag that held the gift-bagged sweaters. Fortunately, the vampires had knitted two spare pink sweaters on the off chance that Alice would have a couple of extra girls at the hen party. I was heartily glad for Sylvia's foresight, as now I had a sweater for Sophie Wynter.

Since we had encouraged Alice to start wearing clothes that fit her better, she seemed to feel more comfortable in her own skin. Alice had dark hair, which she often wore coiled at the back of her neck. It would look severe and formal except for the wispy ringlets that always escaped to curl around her heart-shaped face. Her eyes were clear gray behind her glasses. She had a straight nose, full lips, and beautiful skin. She was, in fact, a beauty and tried to downplay her looks, but her bashfulness somehow only emphasized them.

Polly and Scarlett were the first guests to arrive. We'd all grown to be close friends when we worked together on a college production of A Midsummer Night's Dream. They seemed truly happy for Alice, hugging her and asking if she was nervous.

"I'm not nervous about marrying Charlie. It's a dream come true. It's when I wake up in the middle of the night and worry that I've dreamed my engagement that I get nervous."

Scarlett laughed. "Sounds like true love to me. And you don't need to worry about Charlie. He's crazy about you."

We'd ordered pitchers of sangria and soft drinks, and we started the evening by clinking glasses of sangria.

More women began arriving. I didn't know many of them. They were friends of Alice's and, in a few cases, of Charlie's.

Sophie Wynter was one of the last to arrive. She looked around at the giggling gathering of women and paused on the threshold, her eyebrows raised slightly. Something about her entrance cast a chill into the air. It reminded me a little of when Margaret Twigg took her place at the head of our coven of witches. She was a powerful witch, but she was also a bit mean and definitely condescending to me. Sophie Wynter had that way about her, as though she'd stumbled into the wrong room and was meant to be with much more interesting people.

For a second, everyone stared at the woman standing at the entrance, and then Alice went to her. "Sophie, I'm so pleased to see you. Come on in and meet everybody."

Liva, a Danish woman who had dated Charlie during university and returned for the wedding with husband and baby in tow, rose and went forward. "Why, Sophie, it's so nice to see you again."

Apart from a slight crispness to her words, Liva had almost no discernible accent. Sophie didn't look particularly pleased to see her, but they air-kissed on both cheeks European-style anyway. The two women seemed friendly enough, but there was a strange energy between them. In fact, since I had first seen Sophie, my witch senses had been tingling. It was like a low-grade alarm. I made a mental note to keep an eye on her. Since my love potion had helped to bring Alice and Charlie together, I felt a vested interest in the success of the whole enterprise. I wasn't going to let some cold-looking woman with hard edges slice Alice's happiness to ribbons, and my intuition said that's what Sophie Wynter had in mind.

For the moment, she and Liva seemed happy speaking together. Liva hadn't known too many people, and I didn't get the feeling that Sophie knew anyone at all, so at least they had each other. By reaching over and offering them the jug of sangria, I was able to overhear that they were talking about a weekend Liva had spent in Wembley where she and Charlie had spent time with Sophie and Boris. That seemed innocuous enough.

"How long ago that seems," Liva said. "I don't know if you

remember, but I fell ill with the most terrible flu that weekend. I'm afraid it rather put me off Wembley."

"It should have put you off Charlie," Sophie said.

Liva looked puzzled. "But he was so kind to me. It only made me like him more."

Sophie looked suddenly furious. "Well, you and Charlie didn't last, did you?"

"No. We were not meant for each other. And now I have the right man, and I'm very happy Charlie has found his perfect woman." Liva glanced at Alice, laughing with her friends, and there was affection in her eyes. But when Sophie's gaze followed hers, the expression in them was so cold, I nearly shivered.

Now that everyone had arrived, Violet and I handed out the gift bags. All the girls looked delighted as they unwrapped their cardigans and immediately put them on. I was really pleased to be able to offer Sophie one as well, so she'd feel welcome and hopefully try to fit in and park the attitude. When I gave her the gift bag, she was momentarily surprised. She opened it and pulled out the sweater. "Oh. I hadn't thought." She turned it over in her hands and didn't put hers on. As though I were looking at it through her eyes, I saw that the bride and groom buttons were cheap plastic, and the way the words Charlie and Alice and the wedding date had been knitted into the sweater looked homespun.

Perhaps I was being unkind and she was only feeling embarrassed, as she knew she hadn't been expected. So I reassured her. "It should fit. They're basically one-size-fits-all." She still stared at the sweater as though unsure what to do with it. "Alice is so pleased you could make it. We don't have too many of Charlie's friends here."

A bolt of something very much like fury went across the surface of her blue eyes. "Friend?" The word dripped with significance. "*Friend* of Charlie?" She stared at me as though I were on one of those awful game shows and I'd given the wrong answer. I was about to be voted off the island, laughed off the stage, tossed out the window. Then she gave a brittle laugh. "Oh yes, Charlie and I are good friends."

Liva glanced at me and then back at Sophie. "You must try on the sweater. They're so pretty. And in Alice's wedding color too, I understand."

Sophie turned up her nose. "Pale pink. How perfect. If you're a baby."

Fortunately, Alice was happily chattering to some of her old school friends and had no idea that Sophie was being disparaging. I didn't know what to do, so I gave a helpless look to Liva, who gave me a small nod in return. I took that to mean, "Don't worry, I'll take care of her." I hoped that was what she meant, because I intended to let her.

I was getting a bad feeling about Sophie Wynter. A very bad feeling.

CHAPTER 3

*L*arge plates of food began to arrive. There were huge dishes of paella, meat, fish and vegetarian options. There were plates of tapas, olives, cheeses and charcuterie and thick, crusty bread.

Also salads and cut-up vegetables. Basically, every possible dietary restriction we could think of, we'd accommodated.

I settled myself beside Violet and kept half an eye on Sophie. Under the noise of fifteen women laughing and having a good time, I rapidly explained to Vi about Sophie's odd behavior. "Are you feeling anything from her?" I wasn't always sure of myself, as I was still new at the witch thing. Violet had known she was a witch all her life so was more practiced in her craft.

My cousin looked puzzled. "Why did she want to come to his wedding if she wasn't his friend?"

I sighed. "You've seen Charlie. He's absolutely gorgeous, but I suspect half the time he doesn't have any clue when women are in love with him. Well, look at Alice. Maybe it happened before."

Violet reached for another scoop of paella. "I'm never going to get into my bridesmaid dress if I don't stop eating this. It's so good." She balanced a prawn precariously on top of her mound of rice and vegetables. "So you think Sophie might've had a little crush on Charlie?"

"Maybe. Her reaction was certainly odd."

She looked down the table to where Sophie sat, not eating anything, and the only person not wearing the cardigan. "He and her brother Boris are old friends. Maybe she came to keep her brother company? Maybe it wasn't that she liked Charlie too much but that she didn't like him at all."

"Maybe." I'd be keeping an eye on Sophie Wynter in any case.

After we'd eaten our fill and drunk more of the sangria than was probably good for a group of women who were about to go out drinking, little groups of two or three women at a time took turns going down to the bathrooms to tidy ourselves and repair makeup. Then it was time to head out.

We got Beatrice to present the tiara to Alice. When the bride-to-be demurred, Beatrice put one hand on her hip and with the other pushed the tasteful tiara at the bride. "If it'd been up to me? You'd be wearing a huge plastic tiara with a battery pack so the jewels would light up. You'd also be wearing a plastic ball and chain and one of those huge sashes that says Bride. I found one that lights up." She looked around with a rather evil look on her face. "I've got all of those things in my hotel room. It won't take a minute to get them."

Alice burst out laughing and reached for the small,

tasteful tiara. "No. Please, anything but that. I promise to wear this nice tiara."

Beatrice didn't let her off the hook so easily. "And you promise not to take it off?"

"Not unless I'm held to ransom."

"All right then." Beatrice appeared slightly tipsy as she threw a hand in the air and made a motion like a cowgirl about to lasso a horse. Or a cowboy. "All right, ladies? Let's go."

It was a lovely, warm evening, so apart from the sweaters, all most of us had with us were our handbags. From the tapas restaurant it wasn't very far to our first port of call—The Turf Tavern. Beatrice and Violet walked up front with Alice, leading the way, and I decided to bring up the rear, rather like a border collie keeping my flock together. I was determined that we should at least manage to stay together for the first pub. After that, somebody else could nip at the heels of any reluctant hens.

We walked under Oxford's Bridge of Sighs, then headed down the narrow alley that led to one of my favorite pubs. The Turf was ancient, with a series of interconnecting rooms. It was popular with locals and tourists. As we were heading in, a group of women were heading out. It was clearly a rival hen party. The bride was wearing a plastic tiara with battery-powered lights. A pink plastic sash that said Bride lit up her middle. She wore a skintight dress and the highest heels I'd ever seen. They were so high, I didn't know how she didn't pitch forward on her face. She took one look at Alice and shrieked, "My sister bride!" And then she threw her arms around Alice, and the way the heels tipped her forward, the pair of them staggered, she falling forward and Alice backward. The rest of the hen party laughed and welcomed us.

"We just got the place warmed up for you," one of them said. "Love your cardies."

Then they gathered up their bride and headed off down the street. One of them turned to yell, "Probably see you all later."

I used to think of Oxford as a very serious, intellectual place, but that was before I lived here. I then discovered that it was one of the most popular destinations for hen parties. Oxford was so beautiful, who wouldn't want to spend a weekend here? It also featured a nice, walkable center with lots of pubs. Groups of brides and their women friends came from all over for hen weekends.

Of course, groups of young men also quite liked Oxford for their stag parties.

Briefly, I wondered how Charlie was making out tonight. He'd insisted he only wanted a quiet dinner with some of his closest male friends, but I couldn't imagine that they wouldn't end up turning the quiet evening into one of revelry, especially since I'd met Boris.

We'd already arranged to have a tab set up at this bar, but Alice went straight up to the bartender and said, "I want to open a tab. These are all my friends. I'm buying them a drink to celebrate my wedding."

Alice had drunk about two sips of the champagne at my place and all of one glass of sangria, and she appeared to be the worse for wear. Alice, I feared, was not a drinker. However, the bartenders here were pretty used to partying brides, and all he said was, "Happy to oblige." And then he motioned to the two tables that Violet and I had already reserved. Not that I thought we'd stay in them for very long, but it was nice to have a place to settle and put our bags and chat for a bit. Violet and I were going to encourage all the women to change places at every pub so that everybody met everybody else.

We waited until everyone was sitting and then, as soon as the first drinks had arrived, we got everyone to stand up and reseat themselves in order of how long they'd known Alice. It was a great icebreaker, as we all then tried to work out when we'd first met Alice, and there was lots of laughing and changing places. This put Alice's cousin Ginny on one side of Alice, as she'd indisputably known her longest, and Sophie, who'd only met the bride an hour before the hen party, on her other side as the one who'd known her the shortest amount of time.

Beatrice stood up. She said, "Now, while it's early and we can still make our tongues behave, I want to go around the table and each of us tell how they met Alice and one thing about her."

"Oh, that's a great idea," Ginny said. "Because I'm her cousin and I've known Alice the longest, I think it's only fair that I should start."

Alice already looked embarrassed. Ginny was ten or fifteen years older than her cousin and seemed very patronizing. "Please, don't tell some mortifying story about when I was a baby."

She shook her head. "Alice, the most wonderful thing about you is I don't think there are any embarrassing stories." She turned to the rest of us. "Alice was always well behaved as a little girl. She loved animals, crafts and reading, of course. She was very clever at school. She used to watch my mother knitting. And she said that she wanted to knit too. Mum started her off making a scarf, and Alice worked so carefully, unpicking the thing if she made even the slightest error."

That sounded very much like Alice. A perfectionist in all things.

As we went around the table, we learned that Alice had been a fierce competitor in field hockey and that she'd loved a certain boy band that had us all mocking her fiercely even as I, and I bet most of the other women, privately admitted to having had a similar crush, and even, perhaps, a poster of said boy band on our teenage bedroom walls. When it was my turn, I talked about how Alice taught classes for me in my knitting shop, and she was as patient with her students as she was meticulous with her own work. Okay, it didn't elicit gales of laughter, but it was true, and Alice looked truly touched by my words.

We came around, at last, to Sophie Wynter. She was drinking something that looked like a martini, one of those clear, lethal drinks that are all alcohol. "I've known Alice for the shortest length of time, as I just met her this evening, so I can't tell a story about her, but I can tell you that when I was engaged to Charlie—"

She was interrupted by a gasp of distress. Needless to say, the gasp of distress came from Alice. "Engaged?" Her entire face sagged with shock.

Sophie raised her fine eyebrows. "Oh, dear, I suppose Charlie hasn't told you all his secrets." Then she gave a nasty, superior smirk that made me long to smack her. "Anyway, we went to a charity event, and there were tarot card readings. It was all in fun, but I've never forgotten my reading. The woman said, 'You and your fiancé will travel a twisting road.

27

But you will end up together eventually. It won't be your first marriage, but it will be your happiest.'"

Into the stunned silence, she lifted her drink in a mock toast before sipping.

Ginny said, "Everybody knows fortune-tellers are a bunch of fakes. I once had one tell me I was going to marry a movie star. Well, that didn't happen, did it?"

Unfortunately, now that we'd been split up, I wasn't sitting near Violet anymore. I tried to catch her gaze, but she wasn't having any of it. Violet had done a short stint as a fortune-teller, and she wasn't a fake. Unfortunately, she also wasn't very tactful, and she tended to give people the truth about their future, even if it was negative. This had made her very unpopular at the village fête for Moreton-under-Wychwood. I saw her looking at Sophie Wynter now with an intent gaze. I wasn't sure how her ability to see the future worked, whether she had to touch the person or could simply concentrate on them, but she was staring at Sophie so hard, the woman looked over at her. "Have I got a smudge on my nose or something?"

In a loud voice, Beatrice said, "Okay then, who's next?" Which only showed how rattled she was, because we'd all now shared our reminiscences.

There was a small pause, and then Ginny, who might be a bit annoying but who was also kind, said, "Oh, I remember another story about Alice I think you'll all like." And so the moment passed, and the rest of the women had nothing but kind things to say about Alice and fond, humorous, and sometimes tearful stories of their friend.

Alice kept her smile on her face, but I could tell that she was shocked by what Sophie had said. When it was time to go to the next pub, I made sure to walk beside the bride. In a low voice, I said, "I think you should talk to Charlie. If you ask me, that woman has troublemaker written all over her. No doubt he rejected her and she's just being spiteful and bitter."

Her face was troubled. "Do you think so? We've never really talked about our romantic pasts. Well, I don't have much of one, and Charlie always says it's not relevant. He loves me and he'll always love me." She turned to look at me. "But wouldn't he tell me if he'd been engaged to marry another woman? Especially as he invited her to the wedding."

"Please, just try to have a good time tonight. Put all of this out of your head. And then tomorrow, you and Charlie can have a good talk about it."

"Yes, of course you're right." She shook her head. "I'm being silly."

By the time we reached the second pub, I could feel Violet's emotions. They were vibrating, and if I could have painted them, they would have been pulsing with red and black flashes. I held her back from going in and let all the others go ahead of us. In a low, furious voice, she said to me, "I'm going to turn her into a frog. No. Frog is too good for her. Frogs are lovely creatures. Cockroach. I shall turn her into a cockroach."

I didn't have any need to ask her who she was threatening. I was angry with Sophie too, but I didn't think witchcraft was the answer. "You can't turn one of Alice and Charlie's wedding guests into an insect. People will talk."

The red and black aura lost some of the spiking around its edges. "I know." She tossed her long, dark hair over her shoulder. She liked to dye a ribbon of hair down one side of her face, and in honor of Alice's special day, the stripe was pink. Perhaps a slightly more garish pink than Alice had chosen. "Fine. But if a large glass of red wine accidentally spills itself down her dress, don't be surprised."

I thought I could live with that, and so we agreed that should Sophie Wynter suffer an unfortunate wine-related accident, I wouldn't say a word. Mainly because it would get her out of the hen party, and then perhaps Alice could go back to having a good time.

"You were looking at Sophie very intently when she talked about that fortune-teller. Did you see something?"

Vi made a back-and-forth motion with her hand. "I saw her at a wedding. She was definitely the bride. But the groom was fuzzy. Could have been Charlie, but it could also have been any white man about his age with brown hair. I couldn't bring him into focus."

"I think our job is to make sure that horrible woman never gets Charlie in her clutches. For his sake as well as Alice's."

"Agreed." She looked at me from under her lashes. "You're sure you won't reconsider the cockroach?"

The Eagle and Child pub was a bit of a walk, but since Alice loved books, and this had been the haunt of Tolkien and C.S. Lewis, among others, we'd had to include it. However, there was a rugby team in the big room at the back where we ended up, and our flock of hens began to scatter.

One of the rugby players attempted to talk to Sophie, but whatever she replied had him scampering off with his tail between his legs. I decided to sit beside her and see what I could find out about her alleged engagement. Alice was upset, and as one of her bridesmaids, I felt it was my job to keep this wedding running smoothly. Besides, I was curious. Had Charlie really been engaged to this icicle?

Using my friendliest tone, I said, "I haven't really had a chance to get to know you." I took the seat beside her, and she seemed unconcerned as to whether I sat there or not. "I think you said you went to school with Charlie?"

She looked at me coldly. "My brother went to school with Charlie. I'm a few years younger than Boris, and I met Charlie through him."

Well, if she could be cold and direct, so could I. "And you were engaged to him?"

Suddenly, her cold face grew warm and animated. The transformation was quite astonishing. She looked younger and much nicer. "Yes, I was. And I will be again. Make no mistake. Charlie loves me. I'm sure this whole engagement was a stunt to get me back." She glanced at Alice, who was listening quietly to her cousin Ginny. They were drinking tea. Alice's glasses slipped a little and she pushed them back up her nose with one finger. "Look at her. She's like a Victoria sponge. All soft and sweet with nothing in the middle but jam."

I was furious on Alice's behalf. There was more to the bride-to-be than met the eye. Anyway, who wouldn't prefer a Victoria sponge to a cold, hard icicle?

In a bright voice, I said, "Well, I don't think he's bluffing. I think that Charlie and Alice are going to get married at the church in Moreton-under-Wychwood on Saturday." I left the rest unspoken. *And there's nothing you can do about it.*

She was still gazing at Alice, but her face went hard. "I wouldn't be too sure of that."

CHAPTER 4

J woke up the next morning and my first thought was of water. I longed for a very tall glass. Preferably ice-cold. It was that thought that got me out of bed. I wasn't exactly hungover, but as I downed that long, cool glass of water, I wondered if that last drink at that last pub last night might have been a mistake.

Still, I'd survived my first hen party. Enjoyed it even. Mostly.

I put the coffee on and while it was brewing, Nyx came in looking for her breakfast. Her black fur was sleek and shiny, and she looked pleased with herself, as though she'd enjoyed a very successful night out and was definitely in the mood for a fresh can of tuna. She meowed piteously as though she were one can of tuna away from death by starvation. I got the can opener, and as the smell of tuna assailed my nostrils, I groaned. Perhaps the last two drinks had been mistakes.

"Tuna? First thing in the morning? Really, Nyx?"

My cat had no sympathy for my delicate state and

meowed again. Behind me, Violet's voice complained, "Pussy-cat, do you have to make that dreadful racket?"

I turned and suppressed a grin. My cousin Violet was definitely the worse for wear. Her long, black hair looked tangled, as though she'd spent the night running through dense fields of brambles. Her eyes were smudgy with cosmetics where she hadn't washed her face properly when she went to bed. Her eyes were puffy and her skin sallow.

"You look terrible," I said.

"Feel worse."

I put Nyx's tuna down, and the cat dove in. "I've got coffee on."

Violet went straight to the cupboard where my grand-mother had kept all her herbs and I had freshened up the supply. She shook her head at me. "Haven't you heard the term *witch doctor?*"

I didn't entirely approve of the way she was rifling through my precious herbs. "You're going to make a magic spell for a hangover?" My tone made it clear I wasn't convinced this was the best use of our craft.

"I shall make us a special tea that improves the energy," she said virtuously. "Curing a hangover is merely a side benefit."

She pulled out lemon balm, dried ginger, three different kinds of mint and some herbs I didn't recognize. I set the kettle to boil while she poured various herbs into a ceramic bowl. There was an awful lot there for one pot of tea. She must be really hungover. When she was satisfied, she mixed the whole lot together, and then placing her hand above the herbs and moving it in a circular pattern over top, she said, "Herbs for healing and energy true, bring us to health with this earthly brew. Take away what's toxic and purify with this tea. So I will, so mote it be."

Then she dug around in the cupboard until she found an empty tin that had once held chamomile tea bags. Carefully, she poured the mixture inside. "Don't forget to label this. It's good for headaches, indigestion—"

"And hangovers."

She stared at me. "Do you want some or not?"

"I suppose I could try some, for the energy," I said airily.

The tea tasted really good. I recognized the ginger and mint, as their flavors were strong. I closed my eyes and rolled the brew over my tongue like a sommelier tasting the finest wine. "Is there some ginkgo in there?"

Violet sent me a sly look. "Secret family recipe."

I'd look in my grimoire. I'd bet that recipe or one very similar to it was in our family spell book. Violet was just annoyed because I was the one who'd ended up with the spell book and not her.

We drank our tea and then I downed a cup of coffee for good measure. Nyx finished her whole bowl of tuna and lapped a little water before strolling into the living room and jumping up on the couch. She found a shaft of sunlight and curled herself up in it, ready for her post-breakfast snooze.

I opened the fridge, wondering if sometime in the night some magical creature had slipped into the kitchen and stocked it full of enticing delicacies, but no. This was the fridge of a single woman who didn't do a lot of cooking. I looked at Violet. "I've got some eggs. Cheese. Half a loaf of bread. I could do scrambled eggs and toast. I think there's some cereal in the cupboard."

"Why don't we go next door to Elderflower Tea Shop?"

I thought that tea was really working. It had certainly sharpened Violet's brain so she came up with this excellent idea. We went off to shower and dress and then headed out. I wore jeans with a silky poppy-colored sweater that Theodore had knit for me. I tried to take turns wearing the gifts from my vampire knitters so none of them ever felt they weren't appreciated. It could be a little trying when it came to Mabel, as she tended to knit things that would have looked great if I were a fifties housewife.

However, Theodore knitted from my current stock of patterns and usually asked me first if I liked something before going ahead and making it. We'd chosen this wool together, and this was the first time I'd worn the sweater.

Violet wore a tight black skirt and a slouchy purple sweater that she'd knit herself. Unlike me, she was an excellent knitter.

Elderflower was only next door, so we didn't have far to go, but before we made it, I saw a curious sight. Across the street and up a little way from Cardinal Woolsey's was Frogg's Books. Standing in front of the window were Alice and Beatrice, and they were giggling. I'd have called out to them, but neither Violet nor I needed loud noise in our lives right now. Instead, I tugged on Violet's arm, and we crossed the street to join the two laughing women. It crossed my mind that they might still be inebriated, but Alice at least had seemed perfectly lucid by the end of last night's party.

In fact, Sophie Wynter announcing that she was going to marry Alice's fiancé had acted like a combination of a freezing cold shower and a couple of cups of black coffee to instantly sober Alice up. After that, Alice had stuck to tea, and I wondered if she'd wanted to keep a cool head so as not to say or do anything she might later regret.

Sophie's inappropriate behavior hadn't ruined the night, but it had certainly put a bit of a damper on the festivities. Though the evening had improved when a glass of red wine fell into her lap. She'd shrieked and jumped out of her seat. She'd immediately jerked her entire body around trying to find someone to blame, but no one was standing near her at the time.

I'd glanced around to find Violet standing a few feet away, looking pleased with herself. After Sophie left, the party got a lot more fun.

I was about to ask them what was so funny when I peered through the window. Then I didn't need to ask. Charlie was sound asleep in one of the comfy chairs reserved for bookstore patrons. He was still dressed in black trousers and the white shirt he'd worn out to dinner last night.

He looked as though he'd spent an uncomfortable night and ended up with his head on one of the stuffed armrests, while his legs were jammed against one of the bookcases, presumably to stop him sliding out of the chair and onto the floor. One of his arms was up over the back of the chair, clinging on.

"That quiet, elegant dinner last night must have ended early," Violet said.

Whether he heard the four of us laughing at him or felt our scrutiny or just woke up, his eyes blinked a few times, and then he sat up and rubbed his hands over his face.

He waved one hand our way, and then he stood up very slowly. I suspected that Charlie was in urgent need of some of Violet's magic tea.

He staggered to his feet and walked slowly to the door and let us in.

"Why are you sleeping in the shop?" Beatrice asked him.

He looked around as though surprised to find himself there. "I have no idea."

Alice said, "I'll make you some tea."

His face twisted in pain. "Not sure I could face it."

I glanced at Violet, who nodded her understanding. "I've got some special hangover tea. I'll just run back to Lucy's and get it."

I slipped her my key, and she headed back out. Beatrice, who wasn't as understanding as Alice, said, "I thought you were going for a quiet dinner last night?"

He groaned. "I thought so too. It started out quiet enough. But I think it ended up rather raucous."

He looked around and blinked a few times. "I must change my clothes. Have a shower. Come upstairs."

I was about to say we'd come back later, and Alice was shaking her head, but Beatrice was already halfway upstairs. Alice looked at me and shrugged, and so we followed Charlie up.

When he opened the door to his apartment above the bookstore, it became apparent why he'd slept downstairs. His flat appeared to be full of bodies. Possibly dead ones.

One guy was sprawled across the couch, and another lay on the floor wrapped in a blanket and with his head resting on one of the couch cushions. From the bedroom emerged the most powerful snores I had ever heard.

Charlie stopped for a moment and listened. Then he nodded as though happy to have a puzzle solved. "That's why I went downstairs. The noise."

He looked at us vaguely. "Make yourselves at home. Throw Alistair on the floor so you can sit down."

He went into the bathroom, and I heard the shower go on and then a piercing yell. The shower turned off. A minute later, a stranger came out with his head soaking wet and his white shirt clinging damply to his skin. At the sight of us, he blinked a few times. "Good morning. I was sleeping in the bath." He rubbed the side of his neck. "Mistake." He walked to the stove and took the tea towel hanging from the rail and wiped it over his wet face.

He peered closely at every surface until he found his glasses sitting on top of the fridge. When he slipped them on, his face looked more complete, as though he'd worn glasses for so long, his face couldn't manage without them. He settled the thick lenses more securely on his nose and said, "I'm Nigel Potts. Pleasure to meet you."

An earsplitting snore came from the bedroom. The guy on the couch jumped and cried out, "What? I'm up." Then he came fully awake and saw all of us looking at him. He was a redhead with freckles and large, green eyes. He swiveled and put his feet on the floor. He ran his tongue over dry lips, and I remembered how I had felt first thing this morning. I opened the fridge and found a jug of cold filtered water. I poured a glass and handed it to the guy on the couch, who took it and drank it all down. "You must be an angel," he said to me.

I took the empty glass back. "Refill?"

He nodded. "Let me amend that. You must be the Queen of the Angels."

He sipped this one more slowly. "I dreamed I was in the Old West, I think. I was tied to a train track and a steam train was headed for me." He jerked his head toward the bedroom, where the snoring did sound a bit like a steam train. "Now I know why." He winced. "Can somebody wake him up? It's torture."

Nigel, the soaking wet guy, still holding the tea towel, went into the bedroom. "Hey, Welly," he yelled. "You're snoring."

There were a few snorts, and then the snoring stopped. A deep voice rumbled something, and then Nigel emerged. Following him was possibly the most beautiful man I'd ever seen. He had dark skin, close-cropped black hair, and eyes of a startling blue. No wonder he could snore so loud with that chest. He had to be an athlete. He looked around the room sheepishly. "Was I snoring?"

Nigel threw the tea cloth at his face.

When he smiled, his teeth were white and even. "Ladies," he said.

I think we were all struck speechless, because none of us said a word. Fortunately, Charlie emerged from the bathroom in a navy blue terrycloth robe. His feet were bare and his hair still damp from the shower. He shook his head. "Well, this isn't how I imagined we'd all meet. But this is the wedding party." He toed the sleeping man on the floor. "Except for Giles here. He'd have been a groomsman, if needed, but he'll do a reading instead."

Giles sat up slowly. He had blond, tousled hair and looked delicate, yet he had a glint in his eye as he checked out the bridesmaids that made me suspect he was all grown up.

Beatrice found her voice first. "You're the wedding party?"

Giles chuckled. "You're the bridesmaids?"

It seemed those two approved of each other.

Charlie rubbed his forehead as though he were trying to

massage some sense into it. "Right. Proper introductions." He walked up and put an arm around Alice. "Most important of all, my fiancée, Alice Robinson."

As Nigel said, "You're a lucky man," the guy who'd been sleeping on the couch, Alistair, said, "It's not too late, Alice. Don't throw yourself away on him. Really. I'd be a much better choice."

Alice laughed and blushed, and Charlie said, "Don't be an arse, Alistair. A woman like Alice wouldn't look twice at you if you were giving away free sweets with purchase."

"No. I suppose you're right," said Alistair, which made me like him.

Charlie turned to Beatrice. "This is Alice's friend from childhood, Beatrice. She's the maid of honor." Then he turned to me and Violet. "Lucy is a good friend of both of us. She runs the knitting shop across the street. Her cousin Violet, also a good friend, works with Lucy."

We both said hello, and Violet put the kettle on.

"The chap on the couch is Alistair Grendell-Smythe. He's my friend from childhood and my best man. Nigel Potts is the wet one."

We all chuckled. In England, calling someone wet was like calling them stupid or dull. I was impressed that Charlie could be that hung over and still make jokes. "The man with the incredible snore is Wellesley Clark, and the fellow on the floor is Giles Brighouse. We grew up near each other, in Wembley, and were all up at Oxford together."

This seemed like a good opportunity for us to get to know one another. I said, "Violet and I were just going to go for breakfast. Do you want to join us?"

Violet began passing out mugs of her magic hangover tea. "Drink this first," she advised.

Everyone nodded or said it was a good idea. Nigel said, "I noticed Elderflower Tea Shop is still there. I wonder if the two old ladies still run it."

I would've taken umbrage at hearing my friends the Miss Watts called old ladies except that he said it with such respect. And as they were both over eighty, I supposed they were, in fact, old ladies. I assured him that the two Miss Watts still ran Elderflower.

"We must go there then. Remember how they used to make us those wonderful breakfasts?"

I thought times might've changed. "They mostly do scones and things. Quiche is probably the closest thing you'll get to a breakfast dish."

He looked at Wellesley Clark in an entirely challenging way. "What do you reckon, Welly? Can we still wrap them around our little fingers?"

Wellesley Clark did not look like he had any trouble wrapping any woman in the world around his little finger. "We can only try."

They drank their magic tea and then took turns getting ready. It was surprising how quickly they could go from slovenly and hung over to very presentable.

It occurred to me that in turning his flat into a frat house, Charlie hadn't included Boris. I wondered if the brother had caused as much trouble at boys' night out as Sophie had with the girls?

What was it with those Wynters? And why had Charlie invited them to his wedding?

CHAPTER 5

The nine of us headed out together, and we fell neatly into pairs. Charlie and Alice walked together, obviously, holding hands and catching up, since they hadn't seen each other for hours. Beatrice and Alistair Grendell-Smythe followed. Violet grabbed the delectable Wellesley Clark as though he were a life preserver and she was drowning. That left me bringing up the rear with Nigel and Giles.

"How's your neck?" I asked Nigel. He must have a really bad crick in it after sleeping in the bathtub all night.

He turned his neck from side to side. And then again. He looked at me in surprise. "It's fine. In fact, I feel remarkably well. What was in the tea?"

He was clearly joking, so I laughed. *Ha ha ha.* "Old family recipe."

We walked into Elderflower Tea Shop. I thought the poor Miss Watts would be hard-pressed to remember students from Cardinal College that they couldn't have seen in over a decade. Charlie was thirty-four years old, so his friends must be around that age too. If they'd graduated when they were twenty-two, Florence and Mary Watt hadn't seen them in a dozen years. Well, they saw Charlie regularly, of course, but surely the others would be strangers.

But either the Miss Watts had incredible memories for their customers or Wellesley, Nigel, Charlie, Giles and Alistair really had wrapped the proprietors of Elderflower Tea Shop around their manly fingers. Florence saw them first and gave a little cry. "I can't believe my eyes." She looked at the men, who not an hour ago had been sprawled all over Charlie's flat and bookshop in a hung-over stupor, as though they were VIP guests of the highest order. "Wellesley? Nigel? Giles? And Alistair." She turned and called for her sister. "Mary. You won't believe who's come to visit us."

Her sister bustled out from the kitchen and made just as much of a fuss. She patted Wellesley on his magnificent chest. "I'll never forget how exciting it was when you captained that eight and rowed us to victory."

To the rest of us, she said, "He rowed for England in the Olympics, you know."

"Didn't win, though," Nigel reminded her helpfully. "Came, what, ninth?"

She swatted him. "Ninth best in all the world? I call that a very fine showing indeed."

So Wellesley had been a rower. That explained the broad shoulders and that chest. The men hugged both ladies, and then the sisters welcomed the rest of us less exalted customers. I wasn't a bit surprised when we were shown to the prize table in the window. We had to drag over a second table and add more chairs, but I truly think they would have thrown existing customers out onto the street if they'd had to make room for their special guests. Fortunately, that wasn't necessary, and the customers already there could finish their scones and tea in peace. Or whatever peace remained with a table of nine of us all getting to know one another.

My second shock occurred when Wellesley and crew didn't even have to turn on the charm. Mary looked at him with a twinkle in her eye. "Don't tell me, you want my special breakfast."

Wellesley grinned at her. He had the whitest teeth I'd seen since I'd left the States. "I've thought of nothing else since I left Oxford."

She looked around at us. "Breakfast for all of you?"

"Why not?" Wellesley looked around and we all nodded.

"And tea or coffee?"

We all chose coffee, and soon Mary returned with a couple of big pots and put them on the table. I don't know how they did it, or whether they sent a helper running up to the corner grocery store, but somehow they managed to put on a full English breakfast that wasn't on the menu. We were treated to fried mushrooms, baked beans, bacon, sausages, fried eggs, and black pudding. There were silver racks containing assorted slices of brown and white toast. The toast rack is a peculiar British invention that ensures toast is always cold before it gets to the table.

I couldn't believe it. The Watt sisters had known me my whole life and—not to boast—but I had helped solve a murder that took place in this very tea shop, and they'd never offered me the full English breakfast. I'd never have dared to order off the menu. Still, thanks to the hearty breakfast and Violet's magic tea, our two groups of virtual strangers were soon acting like we were all old friends.

I'd only ever seen Charlie as the owner of a bookstore and as the man who was going to marry Alice, so it was illuminating to see him with guys he'd grown up with and gone to university with. I suspected that for all of them, when they got together, the years dropped away and they felt like undergrads again.

"I'll never forget that party at the rowing club," Alistair said. "You remember, Welly? Where Boris Wynter got so drunk, he tried to take out one of the sculls and fell in the river? Silly fool panicked and nearly drowned."

"Whatever made you invite him to the wedding?" Nigel asked. "He's not really our sort."

Charlie looked uncomfortable. "I couldn't really not invite him. We've been friends since we were boys. I admit we've drifted apart, but he'd have been so hurt not to be invited. I couldn't do it."

I glanced at Alice to see how she was taking this discussion of Sophie's brother. She kept her gaze on her plate and spread marmalade on a piece of toast, making sure she was carefully scraping so it reached every edge and corner.

Wellesley suddenly laughed. "Quite a pair, those Wynters. Do you remember the time Sophie Wynter snuck into the—"

"The girls can't possibly be interested in our old college reminiscences," Charlie said quite firmly.

"Oh, right. Wasn't thinking."

I glanced once more at Alice. Now that every bit of her piece of toast was covered with marmalade, she was spreading it again with her knife, smoothing all the waves and ridges as though she were icing a perfect cake.

Alistair spoke into the sudden, awkward silence. "Boris isn't all bad, though. He visits my dad from time to time.

They'll watch a football game on the telly or go to the pub. I'm very grateful to him and to Giles, here. He gets so lonely. He likes to see the old faces."

"How is your dad?" Charlie asked.

"Not at all the same since we lost Mum. It's just the two of us now." He sliced into his sausage, piled it up with beans. "Appreciate you inviting him to the wedding. It's good for him to get out a bit."

"Of course. I'm only sorry your mum couldn't be here."

None of us women said anything and, clearly realizing that we were in the dark, Alistair said, "Mum died last year of cancer. Dad's completely lost without her. I've been a bit worried about him. He's not acting quite like himself. I can't be there all the time. I work in Birmingham. Anyway, it was good of you and Alice to invite him, Charlie. It's given him something happy to think about, and very kind of your parents to let him sit in their pew right up front like that. It makes him feel like family. Mum always had a soft spot for you."

"Rupert is like family. I'd a soft spot for your mum, too. And her Sunday lunches."

Alistair chuckled. "She used to make her Bakewell Tart especially when you were coming. She knew it was your favorite."

Charlie nodded. "Will you see if you can find the recipe? You can give to Alice." He reached over and touched his fiancée's hand. "If you want to make me a happy man, you'll give me Alistair's mother's Bakewell Tart. Served with custard."

"I'll be sure to remember that, if I ever want to make you

happy." Then she bit into her perfectly marmaladed toast with a decided crunch.

Since Alice had spent the first years she worked for Charlie showing him her love by baking him cakes every day to go with his tea, it must have seemed a reasonable request when he suggested she bake him a tart. He looked at her in a puzzled way. But then, he hadn't been at the hen party. Sophie and Boris's names had come up enough times in this breakfast that Alice was obviously wondering about Charlie and Sophie's past together and why he hadn't told her. I didn't blame her. I was wondering about it myself.

Alice kept her gaze on her plate. Then Wellesley reminded Charlie that they were to pick up their morning suits that afternoon, and the moment was lost in reminders of where they were to meet and when.

When the bill came, Charlie put up his hand for it. Mary put one hand on her hip and waved the bill with her other. "That's a turn up for the books. One of you actually wanting the bill instead of trying to shove it off on someone else."

Wellesley put his own hand in the air. "No. No. This one's mine."

Mary looked around at all of us with a surprised look on her face. "Now they're fighting for the bill. Will wonders never cease?" She winked at me.

Charlie shook his head at Wellesley. "Really. It's mine. You were all nice enough to come to my wedding."

Giles, Alistair and Nigel jumped into the fray, arguing that they should have a chance at the bill too. I could see Alice was getting ready to just hand her credit card to Mary, and that made me feel like I should pay it. But Wellesley simply stood up and, walking around the table, took Mary in his arms and gave her a big smacking kiss on the cheek. He passed a couple of bills. "Will that cover it?"

I had rarely seen Mary shocked, but her jaw dropped. "Welly. That's far too much."

"I'm an investment banker now. I make an obscene amount of money. Besides, I hope this makes up for all the times we were poor students and didn't tip you properly."

She patted his cheek. "You're a lovely boy. You all are."

"I work in banking, too," Giles said, looking put out.

We walked out together calling out our thank-yous. Beatrice said to Wellesley, "Are you by chance single?"

He looked down at her, smiling and not a bit embarrassed, as though he was asked this all the time. "In a committed relationship."

She shrugged, not looking very surprised. "You make an obscene amount of money and you're gorgeous. My hopes weren't high."

We all laughed, and Alice put an arm around her slightly embarrassing friend. "Come on. We've got some last-minute errands to run. We'll see you all at the rehearsal tonight."

In truth, we really didn't have a great deal to do today. Alice was extremely organized. Still, we were all getting our nails done, and so we headed toward the salon where Alice had booked us.

As we walked, I managed to get Alice in conversation. When I thought no one was listening, I asked her if she'd talked to Charlie about Sophie Wynter.

"No. I wanted to, but then they were teasing him about Sophie coming into his room during university, and I didn't want to appear jealous. After all, what he did before he knew me isn't my business."

"It is if it bothers you," I replied.

"Maybe Sophie had too much to drink and didn't mean to say what she did."

She'd seemed stone-cold sober to me. But I was no expert. "The point is, it doesn't matter whether she was drunk or sober. If what she said bothered you, you need to talk to Charlie. You don't want to start your marriage with a cloud hanging over it." Personally, I suspected that Sophie Wynter had fully intended to cast a cloud of doubt over Alice's wedding day. Why else would she have said such a peculiar thing?

"I know you're right. Of course you are. I just feel silly. If Charlie wanted to marry Sophie Wynter, he had plenty of opportunity. I don't want to look like a jealous wife when we aren't even married yet."

"Your trouble is you're too nice for your own good. Because you'd never say something deliberately to hurt another person, you can't believe such people exist."

She chuckled softly. "I'm not a saint, Lucy." She pointed in the window. "And I do love those open-toed sandals. They'll look very nice with my going-away outfit. I was going to wear a pair that I already own, but it would be rather nice to have new shoes."

I liked the trend of her thoughts. A woman who was thinking about her going-away outfit was clearly feeling confident about her marriage. I glanced at my phone to check the time. We had plenty. "Let's go and try them on."

So then, of course, we all had to go into the shoe store. Alice ended up with her sandals, and Beatrice fell in love with a pair of short boots for fall.

I didn't need shoes, but I did find a small handbag that

would look a lot better with my bridesmaid's dress than the straw bag I had intended to use.

Pleased with our purchases, the bridal party continued toward the nail salon.

On the way, we popped into a store that sold cosmetics and all tried on lipsticks until we found a shade that suited all of us and was in the right pink tone to match the bridesmaid dresses. Alice and Beatrice were having their makeup done at the hotel, and then the salon was bringing in a couple of hairdressers to do their hair. She'd invited Violet and me to join in the fun, but I couldn't stand the thought of spending that many hours in the salon. Besides, I wanted to have time to check in with William, Rafe's butler and the caterer for Alice and Charlie's wedding. That task probably should've been left to Beatrice, as she was the maid of honor, but Beatrice didn't know William and I did.

So I agreed to go and get my makeup done in the morning, and then I'd get Sylvia to do my hair. The glamorous vampire always did a wonderful job, better than any hairdresser I'd ever found.

That would give me time to take care of any last-minute questions that William might have and ensure that everything was perfect before Alice arrived. The bride and her attendants would get ready at Crosyer Manor. Alice's father had a friend with an antique Rolls-Royce, and they would pick up Alice. We bridesmaids would be driven in a more modest vehicle, but we would all leave from the Tudor manor house.

We'd feel like royalty.

CHAPTER 6

*A*lice and Charlie couldn't have asked for a more perfect wedding day, I thought that morning as I headed to Rafe's. The only clouds in the sky were a few white puffy ones that looked down benignly like angels blessing their union. Yes, weddings made me think of things like clouds being angels looking down from on high. No doubt all they really meant was that rain was on its way, but I didn't think it was going to come soon enough to cause any problems for Alice and Charlie, not for their wedding here in Moreton-Under-Wychwood or for the reception to be held at Rafe's house afterward.

William was absolutely efficient and so excited about catering the wedding that he been working on it for weeks.

Alice hadn't needed to hire a wedding planner. Between her and William, they'd planned the whole thing and beautifully. Since Rafe's place was closer than mine to the ceremony, I had also taken him up on his offer of a bedroom for the night. I wasn't a big drinker, but it was nice to know I could imbibe freely of the bottles of champagne even now cooling to the perfect temperature without having to worry about transportation home.

Ever the perfect host, however, Rafe had organized a fleet of cars and drivers to transport the wedding guests back to their homes or hotels so everyone could celebrate in style. The drivers were all vampires, but I didn't think anyone needed to know that.

Wellesley had thrown some more of his obscene salary around, booking a suite at a hotel in downtown Oxford where Charlie and the groomsmen would get ready.

Charlie and Alice would spend their wedding night at the Randolph Hotel, a luxurious five-star hotel in Oxford. I was pleased to see that Charlie was pulling out all the stops for his bride. As he should.

Then, after a night of being utterly pampered in the bridal suite, they were heading on a European tour of the most famous libraries in Europe. It might be an odd way to plan a honeymoon for some people, but for Alice and Charlie, who were united in their love of books, it was perfect.

Where other brides swooned over pictures of white sand beaches with palm trees and cool blue water, Alice got excited about the Royal Library of San Lorenzo de El Escorial, near Madrid; Trinity College Library in Dublin; and the National Library of the Czech Republic in Prague. I knew this because I'd seen the photos. I had to admit, if you were a library geek, these were some good ones.

I probably had an hour or so until Alice and the other two bridesmaids arrived. I wanted to check in with William and see Rafe. It would be a busy day, and we wouldn't get much chance to see each other alone. When I arrived at the manor house in my red car that still had the new car smell, it was

William who let me in. He wore an apron and had a smudge of icing on his nose. Other than that, he was his usual impeccable self. "Lucy. How lovely to see you. Do you need me to bring anything in from the car?"

I was dragging my wheeled bag behind me specifically so he wouldn't have to get anything out of the car. "No. Did our dresses get delivered all right?"

"Oh yes. Everything's ready for you ladies upstairs. I was just doing a few of the last-minute things." He looked pleased with himself. "Come and have a look. Let me know what you think."

I knew that if William was in charge, everything would be well in hand, but when he led me to the front parlor that led out to the terrace and the gardens, I drew my breath in on a gasp. I reached out and grasped his arm. "Oh, William. It's beautiful."

My eyes grew misty as I looked at the flower arrangements, the pillar candles in Alice's signature pink and white all waiting to be lit when the evening drew in. Silver and crystal gleamed, and as he led me forward, he opened the French doors wide, and we stepped out onto the terrace. I felt as though I were somewhere magical.

There were round tables dotted throughout the gardens, each holding a tiny arrangement of pink and white roses in a silver holder. All the tablecloths were in her signature pink. There were huge urns filled with flowers on the terrace, and the garden was strung with lights that would twinkle when afternoon turned to evening. The gazebo was set up, ready for dancing under the stars.

William said, as though I didn't already know all the arrangements intimately, "There will be a string quartet playing appropriate mood music in the afternoon. And then, when the evening draws in, they will be replaced by a band for dancing. Alice and Charlie wanted to keep things fairly casual, so the speeches will be held here, where everyone will gather around. They want to keep formalities to a minimum, which I always think is a sensible idea."

I gazed around in rapture. Add in trays of delicious food going back and forth as well as a buffet in the dining room for later, and I couldn't imagine a more perfect wedding reception. Impulsively, I said, "If I ever get married, William, you are definitely going to be my caterer."

He gave me a strange look, and I realized he was thinking about Rafe and me. It was difficult not to think about Rafe and me getting married here, when it was his home. I was growing to love this place as much as he did. However, there were some fairly obvious issues between us, and they weren't anything that a session of premarital counseling could solve. Could I marry a vampire? Could he have his heart broken by losing a mortal woman to age and death?

I thought of Constance Crosyer resting, or not, depending on whether she'd made those beams creak above my head, and wondered, once more, about what his marriage must have been like.

As though by thinking about him we had conjured him, Rafe strolled onto the terrace. "Good afternoon, Lucy. I hope you're pleased. I've been completely neglected the past few weeks while William turned my house into a wedding venue." He sounded grumpy, but I knew how pleased he was to host Alice and Charlie's wedding.

I walked over and kissed him lightly. "It's good for you to mix with people. You can't spend all your life with your nose in a book, you know." As an expert in rare books and manuscripts, Rafe did, in fact, spend most of his life with his nose in a book. Or papyrus scroll or illuminated manuscript, depending on the client. No wonder he and Charlie and Alice got on so well. They were hard-core bibliophiles. I liked books as much as the next person, but my tastes leaned more to the contemporary paperback style of read. I could appreciate that a first edition of Dr. Johnson's dictionary was exciting or that a recently unearthed scroll out of the Dead Sea was an amazing find, but I didn't have the zeal of those three, and I never would.

While I heaped praise on the bashful William, Rafe looked around, agreeing with me. "You've really done a splendid job, William."

I thought his butler would explode from so much praise from a man who gave it rarely. We were interrupted by a cheerful male voice saying, "Don't bother. Put everything away. Change of plans. I can't go through with it."

Since the cheerful tone didn't match the words, I assumed this was yet another example of incomprehensible British humor. Sure enough, Charlie came around the corner looking as excited and happy as a man in love about to marry the woman of his dreams should look.

William shook his head. "You have to go through with it, mate. Or I'll shove all two hundred and twenty handmade shrimp vol-au-vents down your throat. And as many crab puffs."

Male handshaking and backslapping ensued. Once more I realized I would never understand men. Certainly not British ones.

I wasn't quite as pleased to see Charlie as the others were.

"Charlie, what are you doing here? Alice will be here in an hour, and it's bad luck to see the bride on the day of the wedding."

"I know. I checked with Beatrice, and they're still at the hairdresser. I wanted to speak to you, actually." He looked very dapper. He'd obviously had his hair cut and styled, and I suspected a professional shave job. He was wedding-ready but for his morning suit, and he looked gorgeous.

My eyebrows rose at that. "Me?"

"Yes." He looked apologetic. "Take a walk with me?"

Oh, dear. It didn't seem very good when the groom wanted to take a walk with one of the bridesmaids on his wedding day. Still, I tried to act nonchalant as I walked down to the lawn to meet him. "What's up?" I asked as we began to follow the path that led away from the garden and into the woods behind the manor house.

"It's about the hen night," he began, looking over at the sheep grazing happily in a distant field. I got the feeling he was more comfortable looking anywhere but at me.

I tried to keep my tone light. "You know what they say, Charlie, what happens at the hen night stays at the hen night."

Now he did turn to look at me. "Then something did happen?"

"No. It's an expression. Don't you say that here? It's like, 'What happens in Vegas stays in Vegas.'"

He looked utterly confused. "What's Las Vegas got to do with anything? I wish you'd focus, Lucy. I'm serious."

I shook my head. "Sorry. You were saying? The hen night."

"It's just that Alice has been acting a bit odd, rather

distant, since the hen night. Did something happen I should know about? Every time Sophie Wynter's name comes up, Alice gets a strange expression on her face."

I turned to him and put my hands on my hips. "It's not me you should be talking to about this, Charlie. It's Alice. You guys have to live together for the rest of your lives. You need to be able to talk about things."

"I tried to explain about Sophie, but Alice claimed it was all in the past and she wasn't interested."

Oh, Alice. "Of course, she's interested. She just didn't want to seem like she was obsessed with your ex. Don't you understand women at all?"

"Frankly, no."

Well, I didn't understand men, either, so I had some sympathy.

"Sophie Wynter was an unfortunate mistake. Our families knew each other, you see, and Boris and I played together as boys and went to school together. Sophie is a few years younger. I didn't think too much about her until one summer during university. I saw her for the first time in several years, and she had grown into a stunning young woman. Well, you've seen her."

"Yeah, she's a real catch if your taste runs to the cold, cruel type."

"She was famously loathsome to anyone who worked up the courage to ask her out. It was sort of a joke amongst our friends. And then she paid a flattering amount of attention to me and, naturally, I had a go, and when she said yes, I was as surprised as anyone."

I could feel my lip curling up in disdain all on its own. "You went out with her on a dare? Just to see if you could?"

"All right. I'm not proud of it. But remember, I was young. All of about twenty-one. I wasn't dating anyone else at the time. We were together for one summer. And then it ended, and I went back to school." He had a funny look on his face, and I felt there was more to the story that he wasn't telling me.

Okay, maybe what happened at the hen party was supposed to stay at the hen party, but I thought he should know what Sophie had announced to us all. "Charlie, she said she'd been engaged to you."

He didn't look completely shocked by this news, nor did he immediately refute it. He let out a long sigh. "It wasn't serious. We were at a charity event, and there was a fortune-teller. It was all in good fun. But after she'd had her turn with the woman, Sophie told us the fortune-teller had predicted we would get married. I laughed and said, 'Well, I suppose we're engaged then.'"

"You did what?" Oh, he really did not understand women, certainly not young ones who'd fallen hard.

"It was just a joke. I never meant her to take it seriously." He was back looking at the sheep again. "And then she began telling all her friends we were getting married. When I discovered she'd actually been calling venues to book the wedding, well, I put an end to it." His eyes half-closed in remembered pain. "There was a bit of a dreadful scene. I went back to college, and she wrote me a few impassioned letters. She came to see me a few times. Well, she was a nice girl, friend of the family, so I'd take her out for a meal or tea and we'd talk. I tried to let her down gently."

I was not a violent woman, but at that moment, I really

wanted to smack him upside the head. "I have a feeling it didn't work."

He shook his head. "She said she was in love with me and she'd never be able to love anyone else." He threw his hands up in the air. "What was I supposed to do? I was twenty-one years old. I didn't feel the same way. She was a summer romance. To me, it was never anything more."

I couldn't believe he'd forced this woman onto Alice. "Charlie, she told us that the fortune-teller said you might not marry each other the first time around but that you would end up together. Or something like that. Why did you invite her to your wedding?"

In a tone of complete frustration, he said, "I didn't. I invited Boris because we've been friends since childhood. All the invitations say plus guest. How could I have known he would bring his sister as his guest? The plus one was meant for wives or girlfriends. Husbands and boyfriends."

"Did you tell Alice all of that?"

"Well, obviously, I didn't tell her about the engagement or Sophie's subsequent behavior."

"Stalking."

He indicated his agreement with my assessment of the situation by inclining his head. "Partly out of respect for Sophie. One doesn't always want one's youthful humiliations thrown up in one's face."

I may have breached the unspoken privacy rule of the hen party, but I was glad I had. "Well, now that you know that she told everyone at the hen night, including Alice, that you and she were going to end up together, you need to explain it all to your wife-to-be."

He looked mildly panicked. "I can't do it today. You know it's bad luck to see the bride before the wedding."

"I do. I think it might be even worse luck to marry someone who thinks that you withheld a former engagement from them."

"What should I do?" When he turned that helpless, boyish look on me, I was as big a sucker as Alice.

I actually found myself holding my hands out as though they were scales and weighing them up and down as I contemplated what he should do. Court bad luck by seeing Alice before the wedding? Or keep the good luck of not seeing her, but have this thing between them? The best I could come up with was, "Why don't you call her? It's not ideal, but the bad luck rule is definitely about seeing the bride before the wedding. I don't think there's a rule about talking to her. You'll both feel better if you clear the air. You don't want another woman coming between you on your wedding day, especially not one who told everybody at the hen party that she still thinks she's going to end up with you."

He abandoned contemplation of the sheep once more and stared at me. "She said that?"

"Oh yeah. She made it sound like this was a starter marriage and soon you'd see the light, ditch Alice and marry her."

He scratched the back of his neck as though fire ants were running up and down his body. "Oh, this is bad. Appalling even."

"Don't look so worried. Alice loves you. And, unlike Sophie, she's a perfectly sane person. She'll understand."

"Do you really think so?"

I glanced around at the wedding-perfect garden. "She'd

better understand, or there will be an awful lot of crab puffs going to waste."

He looked at the ground as though fascinated by the way strands of ivy climbed lazily up the trunk of an oak tree. "The thing is, Lucy, I've been trying to call Alice. She's not picking up."

"She's probably just busy."

"My fear is that she won't take my call." He looked up at me, and his blue eyes were earnest and somewhat fearful. "I keep having this vision of myself standing at the altar with all the wedding guests looking at me and someone announces my bride has changed her mind." He shuddered. "I just need to hear her voice and explain. If you phone her, I'm sure she'll pick up the phone."

I was pretty sure she'd pick up if I called too. But I didn't like the possibility that she wasn't answering her fiancé's calls. I was in a dilemma. What was the correct bridesmaid etiquette here? I was pretty sure this wasn't in any wedding rulebook.

I debated with myself for a minute. "Here's my decision. I'll call her, and I'll tell her that you're standing here and want to speak to her. It's up to her whether she takes your call."

"You'll tell her I want to explain? That it's not anything like as bad as she seems to think? And please, please, if she's planning to ditch me at the altar, let me know before I end up standing there like a fool."

"I haven't known Alice very long, but everything I know about her says that she would never leave a man standing at the altar looking foolish. She's got the kindest heart of anyone I've ever known."

That made him look more cheerful. "So you don't think she's going to break our engagement?"

"I didn't say that. I'm just saying she wouldn't leave you standing at the altar. She'd never be that cruel."

He looked nervous, and I was starting to worry about poor William and all the wedding preparations and who was going to eat all those shrimp things and the crab puffs. I picked up my phone and hit Alice's number. I held my finger to my lips and looked at Charlie, letting him know that he mustn't say anything until I gave him permission. He seemed to understand, for he nodded and then watched the phone in my hand the way a dog might watch a juicy bone.

Alice answered. "Lucy. You should've come with us to the hairdresser. He's wonderful."

"I'm so pleased. But you know if we added one more person to have her hair done today it would've taken another hour, and besides, I prefer to go to my own stylist." My long, naturally curly hair didn't always behave, but it did for Sylvia. She only had to look at it, and the curls immediately jumped into submission.

I could hear rustling, then she said, "We'll be on our way as soon as they finish with Beatrice. We should be with you in an hour."

Charlie's eyes never left my face, and I could tell he was straining to hear her part of the conversation. I needed to put him out of his misery. "Alice. You're not planning to ditch Charlie at the altar, are you?"

I heard her intake of breath like a gasp. "No. Why would you even think that?"

"Because I've got Charlie with me right now. He says you

won't take his calls and that you've been distant since the hen party."

"Charlie's standing right there?"

"Yes. He wants to talk to you. Alice, I really think you should hear what he has to say. That thing that Sophie Wynter said at your hen party? It wasn't really true."

"You mean they were never engaged?"

"Please, just let Charlie tell his story. He's worried sick that you're going to dump him before the wedding."

"I would never do that. But I am disappointed."

"Well, I don't personally think that anyone should start out their marriage feeling disappointed. So, as your bridesmaid, I strongly recommend you have a conversation and clear the air before you exchange your vows."

There was a moment of silence, and then I heard a soft chuckle. "He's really worried I'm going to leave him at the altar?"

I knew then that everything was going to be all right. I started to grin. "Terrified. He's shaking like a leaf. I swear if you don't put him out of his misery, he's going to start crying."

I thought Charlie should be punished at least a little bit for causing Alice distress. He shook his head at me. He knew what I was doing. "Don't lay it on too thick, Lucy, or she really will dump me for being a wimp."

It was my turn to laugh. I passed him the phone. "I'll be up on the terrace. Bring me my phone when you're done."

As I walked away, I heard Charlie say, "Alice. Darling. You are everything in the world to me."

Yes, I thought, that was the way to start a marriage, with words of love, not unspoken resentments. I should embroider that on a pillow.

CHAPTER 7

St. John the Divine in Moreton-under-Wychwood looked solemn and timeless in the afternoon light. The village green was busy with children playing and dogs running after balls and each other. It was early September and even though the days were still warm, there was a hint of coolness at night and the sure knowledge that autumn and rain were not far away.

The gardens in the stone cottages along High Street bloomed with dahlias and chrysanthemums and the heavy weight of late-summer roses. It was a beautiful day for a wedding.

Alice and her father were in a vintage Rolls-Royce that a friend had loaned her dad. We three bridesmaids followed in a more modest sedan driven by Alfred, whose long nose beneath his proper chauffeur's cap made him look very distinguished. I'd argued against having a vampire driver, but Alfred had been so anxious to see us all dressed up that I relented. I knew that his chauffeur's cap was made out of technical UV-repelling fabric to protect him from the sun—

still, normally, he'd be sleeping at this time of day. However, he was an excellent driver, and he and Theodore and Christopher Weaver would be driving guests back from Rafe's manor house to their various hotels and homes in the area.

Alfred had picked us up from Rafe's place and been very complimentary about how pretty we looked. I had to agree. We all looked our best. Our pale pink silk gowns were simple and elegant. All of us wore our hair up. Sylvia had outdone herself, and my hair looked tamed but still held my curl. I'd worried a bit that Violet's streak of dyed pink hair might add a garish element, but, in fact, it fit in nicely. Each of us had a modest bouquet of roses and wonderful smelling freesia. I was slightly nervous, as I was the one who had to go first, and in the rehearsal I'd had to practice several times slowing my step so I didn't race to the front.

We pulled up outside and checked to make sure there were no guests who were late stragglers and, seeing none, Alfred got out and opened the rear door for us and then helped us to alight. His hand felt pleasantly cool in the warm late afternoon sunshine. Alice's car was just ahead of us, and her father was helping her tenderly out of the back of the Rolls-Royce.

She straightened and shook out her skirts, and then the driver handed her her bouquet. As I looked at her, I felt my eyes mist. Alice was a beautiful bride. She'd given in to our entreaties to abandon her glasses today and wear contact lenses. Her eyes were stunning. I'd spent so long seeing her hide her light under a bushel that to see her in full makeup, her hair in an up-do, without her glasses and wearing a wedding gown, she looked transformed. I pictured Charlie getting his first glimpse of her and knew that if I kept thinking that way, I was going to ruin my makeup by having a big boo-hoo.

There'd be time for tears later, but now I needed to stay photo-ready. We all fluttered around her, telling her how beautiful she looked.

Alfred had discreetly gotten back into the car to get out of the sunshine, but her human driver was happy to indulge us in a few quick snaps on our phones. I put out my hand and touched her wrist. "Well, this is the moment. Are you ready?"

Her own eyes went teary. "Oh, Lucy. I've been ready for this moment since I first saw Charlie."

"Then let's do this thing. Let's get you married."

We all laughed and then fell into proper order. I eased open the heavy church door to peek inside. Sure enough, all the guests were seated. There was a low buzz of chatter and the rustling of people trying to get comfortable on wooden pews, wearing their best outfits and shoes that no doubt pinched. The usher who'd been on the lookout for me ran back to us. He was Charlie's cousin Walter, all of seventeen and looking very important. "All ready?"

"Good to go."

He made a signal, and the soft harp music stopped and the organ began to play Alice's chosen wedding piece, Pachelbel's Canon. I stepped all the way in and took a moment to breathe. I saw Charlie looking remarkably handsome in morning dress. His three groomsmen were lined up by his side. I remembered to smile and listen to the beat of the music so that I slowed my steps. As I walked up the aisle, I felt the urge to turn and look to my right and found Rafe staring at me with a curious expression on his face. He looked darkly handsome in a lightweight gray summer suit.

He gave me an imperceptible nod as our gazes connected, and then I turned to the front and kept going. Violet followed, then Beatrice, and finally the bride appeared on her father's arm.

By that time, I was in position at the front of the church to see Alice.

The music changed, a signal that the bride was about to walk up the aisle.

When he first saw her, Charlie let out a relieved sigh. And then I heard him say, almost under his breath, "Alice, you're beautiful."

I had a feeling he'd worried right up until this moment that she might not show up. But if there was a bride who looked sure of her groom, it was Alice. Her face was beaming. Everyone in the church rose, and her mother began to cry.

Alice reached the front, and then the ancient wedding service began. Charlie and Alice were not trendy people. There was no writing their own vows business for them. They went with the English Book of Common Prayer service, which was old and beautiful.

The only place they differed from strict tradition was in the reading. Two bookish people, they'd chosen a poem by E.E. Cummings, "I Carry Your Heart With Me." Giles Brighouse came forward. He looked very different from the man I'd first met when he was hung over and sleeping on Charlie's floor. His blond hair was newly styled, his navy suit was perfectly pressed and he read well.

It's a poem about love, of course, and how it seems destined.

The ceiling above me creaked and groaned, but I seemed to be the only one who noticed, so I tried to ignore it by concentrating on the words, which made my own heart ache a little. Love was so easy for some people, and for me, it seemed so complicated.

When he'd finished the reading, Giles picked up the book he'd read from and quietly made his way past the scaffolding to the outside aisle while Beatrice took his place and sang "Ave Maria." As I said, Charlie and Alice were traditional people.

When she'd finished, Beatrice returned and, while Alice whispered her thanks, she also passed her maid of honor her bouquet. Reverend Wallington stepped forward, and the vows began. Once more, I heard the roof groan. Once more, I resisted looking up and listened instead to the vows.

"In sickness and in health, to love and to cherish, till death do us part." I wondered, then, if Rafe and Constance had shared those same vows. No doubt they had, with no idea what their futures held. But Constance had known he was a vampire and she'd taken the risk. Had she been braver than I?

When we got to the part where the minister asked if anyone knew of any reason why they shouldn't get married, I held my breath. I think all of us turned to look at Sophie Wynter, who was garbed all in black and looked like she'd dressed for a funeral rather than a wedding. She held a handkerchief up to her face. She wasn't the only one in the church crying—half the women were dabbing delicately at their eyes —but Sophie Wynter was full-on sobbing.

She sat in the middle of the church, with Liva and her husband on one side and her brother on the other. I saw Boris pass her a clean handkerchief. Then the moment passed, and before I knew it, the minister said those magic words, "I now pronounce you man and wife." I didn't think he said, "You may now kiss the bride," but Charlie took it upon himself to kiss Alice anyway.

I glanced over to see how Sophie took the kiss and discovered she was gone. There was a gap in the pew where she and Boris had been sitting, and when I looked around, I saw the church door just closing.

I'd had an eerie feeling during the entire service. I'd heard the roof groan a few more times, and I began to wonder if the church itself was complaining at having witches and vampires join this congregation of mortals.

Could all of us special creatures hear the wood groaning? As I glanced around, I could see that Violet had nothing but happiness on her face, and Rafe had his eyes half closed as though he were trying not to fall asleep. I suspected I was imagining things, probably because I knew that Rafe's wife had a memorial stone on the wall. His beloved wife.

Charlie turned and shook hands with Alistair, his best man, and was clapped on the back by his groomsmen.

Alice took her bouquet back from Beatrice, and we all helped her turn and readjust her skirts. Then the recessional music began. The organ launched into "The Wedding March" by Mendelssohn. The organist was enthusiastic, and the deep notes made the timbers rattle. At least, my imagination thought so.

Even though we'd practiced the recessional out of the church, there was still a slight delay as we all took our places. We would all walk out in order and then mingle for a little while on the church lawn before heading to Rafe's for the reception. Alice and Charlie were trying to keep things fairly relaxed.

Charlie's parents, with Alistair's father, Rupert, sat on one side of the aisle and Alice's on the other. Rupert Grendell-Smythe's seemed much older than Charlie's parents and perhaps a little confused. As Charlie and Alice began their walk down the aisle, he reached out and clasped the bride's hands, preventing her from heading back down the aisle.

The usher had the doors wide open at the west end of the church, and I could see the sun-dappled lawn and even glimpse the high street. It was like the light at the end of a dark tunnel. My sense of dread grew. I really wanted to get out of here. My feet began to tap in nervous frustration, while Rupert, oblivious to the social cues, talked on. We could all hear him telling her what a beautiful bride she was and how happy she made Charlie.

By this time, the whole congregation was on their feet, clapping. And Rupert kept talking. The recessional music ended and had to start up again from the beginning, and Rupert was still talking. Now, he reminisced about his own wedding day and how much his wife would have loved to be here. Before he could relive his entire, happy marriage, as he seemed inclined to do, Charlie stepped in.

The groom offered his most gracious smile to Alistair's father, said something I didn't hear, and began to lead Alice away.

And that first act of husbandly bossiness saved Alice's life.

$\mathcal{W}$e finally began moving toward the doors when I heard something above my head that sounded like a gunshot or a small explosion and, with a gasp, immediately looked upward.

I saw one of the heavy beams that made up the roof break away and fall. My mind shrieked, "No!" I scrambled for some kind of a spell that would stop the disaster, but it was too late. Even as I registered that the massive beam was falling, it had crashed down, right in the spot where, seconds ago, Alice had been standing talking to Rupert.

Charlie's mother had the presence of mind to throw her body against her husband, pushing them both out of the way, but poor Rupert Grendell-Smythe probably never knew what hit him. One moment he was staring fondly after Charlie and Alice, and the next moment he was gone.

The first seconds after the beam fell were truly terrible. At the back of the church, people were still clapping as though they hadn't clued in that a terrible disaster had occurred. The organ continued to play for a few bars and then suddenly stopped.

A cloud of dust and woodchips bounced, and beneath the beam lay Rupert Grendell-Smythe. He'd been crushed where he stood.

Wellesley pushed Alistair behind him and ran forward.

Reverend Wallington stood as rooted as one of the stone sculptures looking down with placid expressions. And then his lips began to move, though if he was praying, it was too softly for anyone to hear.

Alice and Charlie clung to each other, both white-faced.

I looked down and realized how truly close the bride had come to death. The train of her wedding gown was trapped under the fallen beam. Had she stood there another ten seconds—even five seconds—listening to Rupert, she would have died, too.

As for Rupert Grendell-Smythe, it was immediately clear that he was beyond aid. Still, Wellesley lifted a limp hand and checked the man's pulse. He glanced up at Charlie and shook his head, then gently replaced the man's hand on the church tile. The beam had hit the poor man in the head, and his body lay beneath. His hands reached toward the pulpit. The way he was lying, the soles of his shoes faced upward. I could still see the price tag on the soles. He'd bought new shoes for the wedding.

As the wedding guests realized what had happened, there was a rush for the exit, though some stopped to help the elderly, and parents helped their crying children to safety.

As for the bridal party, we all stood stock-still, and then Alistair suddenly sprang to life, pale and frantic. "Help me. Help me. All of you, help me get this thing off him."

He ran to the beam and began tugging and trying to lift it. Charlie and Wellesley exchanged a glance and both shook their heads. But then they and Nigel went to help. My gaze searched out Rafe. Somehow I felt that he would know what to do. He wasn't where he'd been sitting. As I began to search for him, he was there, at my elbow. "Lucy. You're all right."

I wasn't sure if it was a statement or a question, but I answered, "Yes. But we must get everyone out of here, quickly. It's not safe." I glanced up at the roof, though the groaning seemed to have stopped for now.

The vicar was still standing, praying. Rafe walked up to him. "Reverend Wallington, you must make an announcement. Everyone must leave now. The roof could cave in."

Philip nodded and appeared pleased to have someone tell him what to do. In a voice that was accustomed to making sermons that would reach to the back of a crowded church, he announced, "Ladies and gentlemen. There's been an accident. Please make your way out onto the front lawn. Row by row. As quickly as you can. Go now. God bless you."

Most of the congregation were already leaving as quickly as they could, but there were clusters of people standing as though unsure what to do. Now that they'd been told by the vicar to leave, they also turned and headed for the open doors at the back of the church.

"The police," I said. "Somebody must call the police."

Rafe glanced at the roof. "Let's get you outside first."

I appreciated his concern for me, but I wasn't the only one in danger. The four men, Charlie and his groomsmen, were still struggling with the massive beam. Alice stood there rooted. I realized that my first job as a bridesmaid was to aid the bride. I had to step over the beam in order to reach her. "Rafe. Her skirt's trapped."

He'd been watching the four men heave and sweat, but the ancient beam was thick and heavy, and they didn't so much as budge it. He looked at me and nodded slightly, then stepped forward to help. I had a few spells floating around in my head, but the only one I could think of, if it even worked, would make that beam float up in the air. I didn't think it was a good idea to float massive ancient beams up in the air where everyone could see. I suspected Rafe had a similar problem. He didn't want to lift that beam up as though it weighed nothing, but if we were going to get Alice freed, we would need his superhuman strength.

He leaned down and slipped his hands under the beam, then calmly said, "On three. One, two, three." And they shifted the beam enough that I could pull Alice's dress, and therefore Alice, to safety. Once I'd pulled Alice's skirt free, Alistair tried to lift the beam farther. "Please," he panted. "We have to get Dad."

Rafe stopped him. "There's nothing to be done for your father now. I'm very sorry. Let's all go outside and wait for the police."

All the men stood but Alistair. "I can't leave him. He's got no one but me." He was clearly in shock.

Violet put her arm around him and gently tugged him to his feet. "Your dad would want to know you were safe. He won't be alone for long. Someone will be along very soon."

The minister joined Violet and Alistair, speaking softly. He seemed to have pulled himself together, I was glad to see. The whole bridal party walked out of the now empty church. We were meant to have led the way with joyous celebration.

Instead, we limped down the aisle shaken and filled with shock and grief.

As we emerged, both Charlie's and Alice's parents came rushing up. Alice's mother hugged her. "Oh, my darling. I'm so glad you're all right. When I saw that beam come crashing down, I thought at first you'd been killed."

I gazed around at the wedding guests milling about on the lawn. They stood in small groups—family parties huddling together, couples holding hands. Children held in their mother's arms. Some spoke quietly. Several were crying. I saw Sophie Wynter standing apart with her brother. The woman who'd cried through the whole wedding ceremony now seemed remarkably calm and dry-eyed.

No one seemed to know what to do. I said to the vicar, "Someone should call the police." My handbag was in the car with Alfred. All I had with me was a bouquet of flowers.

He appeared to have the same problem, for he patted his pockets and then shook his head. "I never bring my mobile with me when I'm preaching."

"No. Of course not." I glanced around. Had someone already taken it upon themselves to call the police? It was impossible to tell. Charlie's parents seemed like a sensible pair. I asked them if they had mobile phones with them and if they could call 999. It was clear it hadn't occurred to them. "Yes, of course." His mother opened her bag and found her mobile phone. First she had to turn it on, and then she made the call.

When she'd hung up, she said, "They'll be right over. They've asked that no one leave."

I nodded. Alistair Grendell-Smythe was sitting on the church steps with his hands over his face. Wellesley and

Violet sat on either side of him, offering what comfort they could. I walked up to the pair of ushers, standing together pale-faced. "The police will be here soon. Can you go around and tell everyone they must remain until the police arrive? No one is to leave."

Charlie's cousin Walter, who'd let us in, looked so pale I thought he might pass out. "Blimey. I've never seen anything like it."

And then he straightened his shoulders—"Come on, Eric"—and began to deliver the message.

I didn't know what else to do. Rafe was nowhere to be seen. I didn't think he'd left. No doubt he'd found a shady spot to retire to. With Alice taken up with Charlie, and Violet trying her best to comfort Alistair, I felt at a loss. Beatrice was having hysterics, sobbing in Alice's mother's arms. I didn't feel like crying, and I also didn't feel like talking to people I didn't know. Nigel and Giles stood near Charlie and Alice, but none of them were talking. What was there to say?

I walked up the front path to the stone wall and the gate that led to the high street. How had this happened? What kind of witch was I that I hadn't been able to prevent disaster? I knew what Margaret Twigg would say if I shared my thoughts. "Lucy, we're not magicians. And we're not God." Still, I hated that I had power and I hadn't used it. The accident had happened so fast. One minute, that nice old man was complimenting Alice, and the next minute he was dead. Crushed.

I noticed a couple walking their dog along the high street. It was such an ordinary, everyday activity that I drank in the sight of them. The dog was some kind of terrier and bounded along with his tail wagging and his tongue hanging out.

Watching the foolish puppy and the older couple out walking soothed my troubled spirits. As they grew closer, I realized I recognized them. It was Harry Bloom, a former police detective who'd retired here with his wife, Emily. Even though he no longer worked for the police and was obviously enjoying a Saturday afternoon walk, I waved him over frantically.

He might have been retired, but his instincts were as keen as any detective's. He handed the leash to his wife and strode toward me. "Lucy. Hello, there. Is everything all right?"

He didn't need to be a detective to read trouble in my face or that the crowd mingling in front of the church wasn't a joyous one and this wedding seemed more like a funeral.

Briefly, I told him what had happened. His first question was, "Is everyone out of the church?"

"Yes. Well, except for Rupert Grendell-Smythe."

"He was the victim?" he asked gently.

I nodded.

He put his hand above his eyes to shade them from the sun and looked at the church. "And you're absolutely sure there's no one else in there?"

Was I? "No." I put my hands out in a helpless gesture. "I'm fairly certain there's no one left in the main church. But I suppose there could be other areas of the church." I glanced around. "You'd better ask the vicar. He's over there."

"And you've called the police, I assume?"

"Yes."

As Harry Bloom walked through the gate and strode toward Philip Wallington, I felt immeasurably better. He had an air of authority and plenty of experience in the police. I didn't need to worry so much now that he was here.

His wife arrived at my side. "Lucy. What's happened?"

She might not be a police officer, but she'd been a detective's wife for a long time. Her gaze was almost as sharp as his as she scanned the crowd in front of the church. "Is there anything I can do?" Even the dog seemed to have lost his friskiness, as though he picked up the gloomy atmosphere.

I liked that she hadn't asked any pointed questions. Still, I didn't think the fallen beam was going to remain a secret for long. I told her what had happened. Her free hand went to her chest. "Oh, my goodness. What a terrible way to begin your married life, with a tragedy like that."

I'd been feeling so awful for poor Alistair and Rupert Grendell-Smythe that I'd barely taken the time to realize what this meant for Charlie and Alice. "Oh, my gosh. Their wedding reception."

Poor William. Even now he'd be chilling champagne and putting the last touches on the hors d'oeuvres, checking that the waitstaff's aprons were all pristine and their bowties straight.

She shook her head. "This will cast a shadow over their whole marriage."

"They don't deserve this. They deserve to be happy."

The vicar was talking quietly with her husband. He looked pale and ill. "And poor Philip. We'd only just begun the campaign to raise the funds to replace the roof because of that deathwatch beetle. But the church's restoration committee hired surveyors who said the roof was safe. This is a terrible blow to our whole community."

It was a worse blow for poor Rupert Grendell-Smythe.

I kept thinking about the way I'd heard the beams above me groaning. I didn't want to make this tragedy all about me, but I couldn't help but wonder whether Constance Crosyer could somehow be behind the disaster. There were certainly women who loved men enough that they would kill their rivals, but I had a hard time believing that Rafe would be foolish enough to fall for such a one. But then, of course, he'd had five hundred years or so to get smarter before I met him. Maybe back when he first met Constance, he was young and foolish.

Emily watched her husband talking to the vicar. "I was on the committee that chose Philip Wallington as our vicar, you know. He'd been in Harlesden, I believe it was."

At my raised eyebrows, she said, "It's in London. Not the most savory part." She shook her head. "Philip had worn himself out trying to help solve the problems in that community, and we believed that coming here would be a restful change." The dog pulled on his leash, trying to get to Harry Bloom, but Emily said, "Sit," and good dog that he was, he obediently put his rump on the ground, even as his whole body strained to follow Harry. "What very bad luck. For all of us."

Harry Bloom walked over to Alistair and took Violet's place sitting beside the grieving son. As he sat down, Alistair looked at him intently, his face gray. I thought the retired detective was no doubt explaining the process of what would happen next.

His wife said, "If you'll excuse me, I'll speak to Philip. We'll have to get the word out to the community. Find somewhere else for worship tomorrow." She excused herself, and she and her dog headed toward the beleaguered-looking vicar.

I didn't know where the congregation would gather tomorrow, but it wouldn't be at St. John the Divine.

CHAPTER 9

J looked around for Rafe. I hated to ask him about
his dead wife, but he was the only one still in exis-
tence who'd been around when Constance was alive. Perhaps
if I understood more about her, I could better determine
whether she was a restless spirit who'd go to any lengths to
keep Rafe for herself. I walked around the church and found
him sitting on an ancient stone bench, in the shade of a tree,
overlooking the graveyard.

It was a peaceful spot, with a view of the crumbling gravestones and past that into the village. I doubted this particular
view had changed for hundreds of years. The old cottages,
the twisty lanes, even this tree must be several hundred years
old, based on how thick and gnarly its trunk was.

I had a moment to study Rafe before he saw me. He
looked pensive rather than sad, and as still as one of the
gravestones. I walked forward, and he smiled when he saw
me approaching. When I would've settled beside him on the
bench, he stopped me. He stood up and took off his jacket

and then laid it down on the mottled granite seat. "I wouldn't want you to spoil that pretty frock."

"What about your jacket?"

"It hardly matters. I'm not one of the wedding party."

I sighed. "I don't think my dress much matters either. I suspect this wedding is over."

He nodded. At the same moment, we both said, "Poor William."

Still, I sat on his jacket, and he resumed his place beside me.

"Have you called him?"

Rafe nodded. "But I told him not to send anyone home or put away any food. I suppose anyone who wants to might as well still enjoy the food that William went to so much trouble preparing."

"It won't be a wedding reception. It will be a funeral."

Once more, he nodded.

I licked my lips. Had no idea how to begin a conversation about his dead wife. I looked down at my knees pressed together in my pink silk gown. From a distance, we probably looked like a Victorian couple courting, sitting primly on the stone bench. "Rafe, when I first came into the church, and then again during the service, I thought I could hear noises coming from the roof. Groaning."

His gaze narrowed on my face. "Groaning? You're sure it wasn't a ticking sound?"

"No. More like groaning or creaking. My hearing is better than average, but yours is amazing. Did you hear anything?"

"No. But I wasn't standing right under the faulty beam the way you were."

I felt guilt stab me. Right in the chest. It was an awful feeling. "If only I'd said something, maybe poor Alistair's father would still be alive."

He reached over and took my hand, cool and steady, holding it firmly in his. "And perhaps if the church committee had taken the deathwatch beetle more seriously, Rupert Grendell-Smythe would still be alive and Charlie and Alice's wedding wouldn't be a shambles."

I hadn't thought of that. "So you don't think it's all my fault?"

"I don't think it's your fault at all."

How to even begin to broach the possibility that his dead wife might've tried to kill me with that beam? "I saw the memorial plaque on the wall. To Constance Crosyer."

I kept my voice gentle, but the hand holding mine stiffened suddenly and then deliberately relaxed. "Constance was my wife."

"I'm so sorry. Her loss must seem so fresh to you."

"Well, even the fiercest emotions fade over time, but losing Constance was the greatest tragedy of my life. Even an expected death at the end of a rich life lived to its natural conclusion still leaves grief in its wake. Especially to someone like me. Someone left behind." He paused and looked out over the gravestones, names worn away by time, some fallen over or leaning drunkenly.

"What was she like?" Yes, I was trying to find out whether Constance might've attempted to toss a heavy beam on my head and kill me, but I was also curious. I suppose every woman likes to know about her predecessors.

He took his time choosing his words. "She was one of your kind."

Even though Violet had already told me that Constance had been a witch, I didn't want to let on that we'd been talking about Rafe's business behind his back. I made my tone lilt in surprise. "She was a witch?"

"She was. A very good one. It was a dangerous time for witches then, but she had a gift for healing and couldn't bear to see anyone in pain without trying to help them. It wasn't all witchcraft. She had a genuine healer's touch."

Pretty much the worst thing witches had to deal with these days was mockery. But when Constance had been alive, women were burned and hanged for the crime of witchcraft, and most of the ones put to death hadn't, in fact, been witches at all.

A woman who'd been a healer in life didn't sound like someone who'd suddenly turn into a vengeful ghost. Still, I had to ask. "Was she a jealous woman?"

He laughed softly and shook his head. "Far from it. It wasn't easy for her, as you can imagine. She aged as a normal woman does, while I did not age at all." He looked at me significantly, and I imagined he was letting me know what I was in for if we continued with this relationship. "Then, as now, I was forced to move every decade or so in order to avoid suspicion. Once we had a mob chase us. Not to accuse me of being a vampire but to accuse my wife of witchcraft. They suspected that she had put a spell on me to keep me young forever." His laugh was bitter. "If she could have changed me, I'd have chosen to be mortal with her. But no spell is powerful enough to turn a vampire back into mortal."

He continued to gaze out over the gravestones. "Towards the end, we posed, not as man and wife, but as mother and son. Still, Constance was the love of my very long life." He looked at me. "Until now."

I felt as though I couldn't quite take a breath. I knew he cared for me, but not like this. "I'd wondered if Constance might be angry with me."

His tender look vanished. "You think my wife, who died nearly five hundred years ago, might be a ghost out for vengeance?"

I felt really foolish now. "When I saw her plaque on the wall and then heard the creaking in the rafters, I wondered."

"No. Constance would want me to be happy. She always did. When she grew old, she said she would understand if I looked elsewhere. That she would not only pass herself off as my mother but act like it and welcome her replacement. That's not a woman who would hurt another. If anything, she'd be pleased to know I'd found someone again."

I didn't know what to say. Of course I cared for him. But there was no getting around the fact that I was going to have the same problem Constance had if I stayed with him. He continued, "She'd have liked you. You're very much like her." He paused and then went on, "The first time I saw you, I had a shock. You even look like her."

He wasn't the only one getting a shock. "I look like your dead wife? Who lived in the 1500s?"

"It's not as strange as you might think. Constance had family who moved to Salem, Massachusetts."

"Salem? I'm guessing that didn't end well."

"Don't forget, the actual witches had powers and a very good underground network. Many of them escaped. Your ancestors did."

"My ancestors?"

"Yes. I suspect you are the descendant of Constance's sister."

I put my hands up. "Are you kidding me? I'm having trouble getting my head around that."

He chuckled. "Imagine how I felt when I saw you."

"Kind of blows my theory, then, that your wife was out to get me."

"Constance would want nothing more than to see me happy."

Way to go, Lucy. I'd come out to find out whether his dearly departed wife was my mortal enemy and instead had him all but declaring his undying love for me. And when a vampire expresses undying love, he means it.

Well, at least I no longer had to worry that I had an unhappy ghost out to get me. I was going to have to do something about my undead admirer, though, and I had no idea what that was going to be.

"Even if you weren't part of her family, she'd still look out for you if she could. No, if my wife is a ghost, she's a benign force." He looked around the graveyard, almost sadly. "But I don't believe she walks the earth. I believe she's truly gone."

"So it was really bad luck, then, and nothing more. The poor vicar looked gray, but it seems they have a church restoration committee that hired surveyors. They apparently claimed that the roof was safe enough. The committee thought they had time to raise the funds to replace the damaged parts of the roof. Looks like somebody made a terrible miscalculation."

Rafe turned to me, and his expression was guarded. "I'm not so sure about that."

The bodice of my dress suddenly felt uncomfortably

tight, as though I'd taken a breath and forgotten to let it out. "What do you mean?" I knew that guarded look of his, and it usually meant he was trying to keep bad news from me.

"I'm not entirely sure that falling beam was an accident."

"What?" I shrieked the word so loud a bird flew from a bush, squawking with alarm.

"The beam will need to be carefully studied, but it looked to me as though the ends were rather too neat. Almost as though they'd been cut through."

"Cut through?" I didn't shriek this time, so no wildlife was startled, but still, my voice was urgent. "You mean, deliberately?"

I knew it was a stupid thing to say. The beam couldn't have been cut by accident, but I was completely rattled by Rafe's suspicions. And Rafe wasn't given to scare-mongering.

He didn't call me on the inanity of my reply, merely answered calmly, "I believe so."

"But who? Why?"

"Two excellent questions."

My brain was reeling. "Do you think someone planned to disrupt the wedding and it was a prank gone wrong?"

He considered my question. Then shook his head. "It's much too complicated to be a prank."

"But are you saying that Rupert Grendell-Smythe was murdered?"

"That's exactly what I'm saying."

"Who'd want to kill that nice old man?"

Once more, he seemed to consider my question carefully. "I imagine killing someone by dropping a rotten beam on their head isn't the most accurate method. Perhaps he wasn't the intended victim."

As theories went, I really didn't like this one. "So the real victim is still in danger?"

"Yes."

"But who—" And then I pictured the crash, the horrible thud, the screams, and Alice's dress, the train caught under the broken beam. That's how close she'd been to death. "Alice," I whispered.

"Don't jump to conclusions," he warned me. "It could have been meant for anyone in the immediate vicinity, or perhaps someone had a grudge against the church or the vicar and chose Charlie and Alice's wedding, as the church would be filled with people at a specific time."

"But why not make the beam crash down during a Sunday service? It's just as scheduled, and the church would still be filled with people."

"I can think of several reasons. One, the killer could be someone who'd be missed in church on a Sunday. Two, they could have loved ones in the congregation they wouldn't want harmed, or, three, the church attendance isn't high enough to get the attention and drama they were looking for."

I hated the idea of a madman randomly choosing Alice and Charlie's wedding as a venue to create this horrific disaster, but I hated the prospect that Alice and Charlie had been targeted even more. As bad as a rotten beam randomly falling would have been, it would be preferable to what Rafe was suggesting.

I really wanted to blame the deathwatch beetle!

"Will you tell the police what you suspect?"

"They are trained investigators. I think they'll see for themselves."

I stood up, shook his coat out and offered it back to him.

"I suppose I should see what's going on. See if Alice needs anything."

He stood as well. "The police should be here by now. They'll want to interview everyone, I imagine."

"Poor Alice and Charlie. What a way to start your married life."

"Could have been worse. One of them could have been hit by the beam."

I looked at him sharply. "Alice had been standing, speaking with Rupert Grendell-Smythe moments before the beam fell. You saw her. She was so close, the train of her dress was trapped under the beam." I shuddered. "What a lucky escape."

"I wonder."

I knew what he was thinking. I shook my head. "Don't even go there. It's an old church. We know there's deathwatch beetle in those beams. It could have been an accident."

Maybe if I repeated those words enough, I would believe them.

I didn't want Rafe's theory to be correct, but I also didn't want to hide my head in the sand and possibly leave a woman I liked very much in danger for her life. If there was a killer around, we needed to find them. I looked at Rafe. "Okay, you've obviously thought this through. How did the killer cut the beam through, and how could they be certain it would fall just at that moment?"

"The killer didn't leave too much to chance. I believe they went up into the roof. They'd cut the beam enough that a sharp push would cause it to tumble."

I remembered the sharp gunshot sound I'd heard.

"But how did they get up to the roof?" I looked behind me and saw the tower reaching up into the still-blue sky. "The bell tower?" Then I answered my own question. "But that's impossible. They were going to ring the bells when Alice and Charlie walked out."

I didn't know much about bell towers, now that I thought about it. "Or can people even go up a bell tower?"

He looked amused. "How do you think they rang the bells before modern times? Bells were rung by hand. In fact, many still are. I know people who find it a relaxing hobby. They climb up into the tower and take charge of bell ropes, then pull them in patterns."

A murderous bell-ringer? Now I'd heard everything.

"But I don't think the killer was in the bell tower. It's at the opposite end of the church from the apse."

"Then how did the killer climb up into the roof?" And, suddenly, I knew. "The scaffolding." The church had draped the metal support in blue fabric to hide the ugliness, so the murderer could have climbed up the metal supports and into the roof. Then all they had to do was push the beam down at the right time.

He nodded.

I began to realize why I'd found Rafe sitting out here. He hadn't only been looking for a quiet spot in the shade; he'd been doing some sleuthing.

"But how did they get out?"

"The scaffolding is located in front of the organ, remember?"

"Yes."

"At the bottom of the organ loft is a door to the outside."

He pointed, and I saw a door set into the stone wall of the church. "In the chaos, the killer climbed back down a couple of rungs of the scaffolding, slid down the organ pipe and walked out that door."

And as easy as that, a murderer had walked away.

CHAPTER 10

J went to the door and opened it.

"Don't go in there," Rafe said in a warning tone behind me.

"I won't." But I did stick my head in so I could get an idea of what we were talking about. What I saw was a narrow corridor that led into a rather dark space. I could just glimpse the organ keyboard, though the lights had been turned off, so I couldn't see much. The organ pipes stretched way up, and I wondered if Rafe was right. Could a killer have used them like a fireman's pole to slide down and escape?

And could the murderer really have done it without being seen by the organist? The music would have covered any sound, and I supposed the organist was too busy concentrating on her playing to notice what was going on behind her. Then, when the beam fell, as I recalled, the playing had continued for a while. The organist hadn't been able to see the beam fall.

I came back out of the doorway. "We should tell the police."

"Again, the police aren't stupid. They'll come to the same conclusions we have."

I stood back and regarded this old church. It wasn't only the deathwatch beetle that was slowly destroying the structure. There were patches of moss in places, and a couple of stones had fallen from the wall. They lay on the ground like reminders that time was passing, the same way the writing on so many of those gravestones had worn and washed away over time, leaving it a mystery as to who was buried beneath them.

I'd heard the police arrive and said to Rafe that we should join the others. He motioned me to go on ahead. When I walked back around to the front of the church, the scene hadn't changed very much. Except that now there were several police cars lined up. I recognized Detective Inspector Ian Chisholm, his reddish-blond hair catching the light as he bent to listen to Beatrice, who seemed to have worked herself up into hysterics again. Another officer I recognized, Sergeant Barnes, was talking with Alistair. Harry Bloom stood with his wife and Philip Wallington. He seemed unsure as to whether he should stay or go. Their dog sat gazing up as though wondering as well which way his master was going to go.

An ambulance was parked out front, and two paramedics stood outside the church with the stretcher. I wondered why they didn't go in.

Violet caught sight of me and came over. "Ian Chisholm was looking for you."

I was about to make my way over to him when the fire brigade showed up. Then I understood why the paramedics hadn't gone inside the church. No doubt the police had decreed that no one could enter until the fire department got there. They had the kind of equipment for unstable structures. And, as had been evidenced this morning, this church was clearly unstable.

In the end, it wasn't Ian but a uniformed constable who took my statement. I admitted that I had thought I'd heard creaking in the beams, but nothing that had led me to believe the roof was about to cave in. "It was more like when you walk across the floor and hit a squeaky bit."

Nigel Potts came up to me. He repositioned his glasses, not that he needed to, but I suspected it was a nervous gesture. He was to have been my escort back down the aisle if the wedding had followed protocol. "I'm awfully sorry, Lucy, but I won't be able to escort you to the reception. Alistair has to go and make a formal identification of his father. I said I'd go with him."

"Yes. Of course. Does Alistair mind very much if we still offer the wedding guests food?"

"No. He insisted that Charlie and Alice go ahead. He said it's what his father would've wanted. And I imagine that's true. Rupert loved a party."

I felt my eyes prickle at the death of this man I barely even knew. A man who'd bought brand-new shoes to come to the wedding.

"Of course."

Then Philip Wallington left the Blooms. He stepped up onto a flat-topped stone that edged the walk up to the church door. It was a makeshift pulpit, but it allowed him to see and be seen. He still looked shaken, but he managed to sound calm and in control as he called for attention. Everyone stopped talking and gathered around him, as though grateful that here was someone who would tell them what to do. How to go on.

"Alice and Charlie, friends. God does indeed move in mysterious ways. Who can say why Rupert Grendell-Smythe was taken from us so cruelly and so suddenly today? In the midst of great joy, we now experience great sorrow. Our thoughts are with his son, Alistair, and all his family and loved ones. Let us pray."

It was a short, moving prayer. Then he said, "Charlie and Alice, with Alistair Grendell-Smythe's blessing, have asked me to tell you all that they would be glad to see you, as planned, at Crosyer Manor. And the police have asked me to let you know that you're all now free to leave. God bless you all."

Everyone turned back to whatever group they'd been part of and began to talk. Behind me, I heard an older woman say, "I don't know. Should we go? Seems a bit macabre." I didn't know the speaker, but I turned immediately to a couple who stood, uncertain. No doubt they were family friends of bride or groom and had traveled a fair way for the wedding. "Please," I said, feeling that my bridesmaid dress gave me some right to intrude. "Please come. The caterers have done such a wonderful job. It would be terrible to see all that lovely food go to waste. I believe that Mr. Grendell-Smythe would want Alice and Charlie to have their friends and family around them at this time."

The woman, peering at me from under a large, pale blue hat, looked grateful for my interference. "All right, dear. I suppose it's best."

Surprisingly enough, the vicar came to Charlie and Alice's wedding reception. He looked gray. Was it the normal pallor of a man who's had a shock? Or was there guilt involved? I didn't want to think of the nice vicar as someone who had enemies, but if someone had deliberately tampered with that beam, then Rafe might be right. It could be the church itself or the vicar in particular who had been the real target. This felt like the early hours after a terrorist attack. I found myself waiting for someone to claim responsibility.

As they had in the churchyard, the people who came to Rafe's house tended to stay in groups of people they knew, as though they could find safety that way. Or maybe it was just comfort they were looking for. The vicar went from group to group offering sympathy. At one point, he was standing by himself, and I decided to get to know him a little bit better. I was no longer here as a bridesmaid. I had changed roles to that of amateur sleuth.

I just kept that to myself. I suspected people would talk more freely to a bridesmaid in a pink dress than they might, say, to the police.

I approached the vicar. He smiled at me in a tired fashion, and I could almost see him girding up for a tearful interview. Perhaps he thought I'd throw myself on his chest, sobbing, as I'd seen Beatrice do. Not that she could help it. She was obviously more emotional and, almost certainly, less accustomed to sudden and mysterious death than I was.

Had anyone offered the vicar any sympathy? He was another victim in today's tragedy. To have a suspicious death occur during his wedding service was a terrible blow both to the church and, I suspected, to him. Would he always wonder how things would have turned out if only he'd spoken a little faster? Begun the service two or three minutes earlier?

But, of course, if Rafe was right and there was nothing

accidental about the falling beam, then likely that wouldn't have mattered in the end. Someone would still be lying dead in the church.

"Philip. How are you holding up?" I asked him. Since no doubt he'd been the one offering sympathy so far this afternoon, he blinked in shock at my words. He seemed to gather his thoughts.

"How kind of you to ask." I could see him dredging through the names for mine. "It's Lucy, isn't it?"

Even in tragedy, he had quick recall. I was impressed. "Yes. That's right." I gestured to my dress. "One of the bridesmaids."

"What a sad and tragic event. Alice is fortunate to have good friends to turn to at such a time of crisis." That sounded like a line he'd delivered any number of times in the last couple of hours.

"Philip, I've watched you ministering all afternoon. Do you have friends who will support you? I think this will be a difficult time for you, too."

Did he start slightly? It wasn't that he looked guilty so much as surprised. Had it not occurred to him that his church would be closed for some time and awkward questions would no doubt be asked? I wasn't entirely sure how the clerical hierarchy worked, but I suspected he held a position of authority within his parish and probably had made the final decision on whether the church would continue to operate while the funds were raised to repair the roof. I wondered if that beam would kill his career as surely as it had killed Rupert Grendell-Smythe.

"It's a terrible tragedy, of course. But who can truly understand God's plan?"

"Have you been at St. John the Divine for long?"

Once more, he seemed startled by the question. "Not so very long. Just over two years. I don't think you're one of my parishioners?"

"No. I live in Oxford."

"I was very happy to receive the call to relocate to Moreton-under-Wychwood."

"It must be a nice, quiet life." He was fairly young. I wondered if he ever got bored.

"Not always," he said with an ironic twist to his mouth, and in spite of myself, I laughed. He had a sense of humor.

"I was in London before this, so the change did take some getting used to. Every flock has its personality."

I thought that getting moved from London to the wilds of Oxfordshire wouldn't be considered a promotion in most industries. Quite the opposite. Was it true in the Anglican Church? And if he'd been demoted, I had to wonder why. Emily Bloom had suggested burnout, but I wondered.

How to ask that without seeming to? I wasn't always the most subtle of people, plus, being North American, I tended to be more direct than most Brits. I settled on, "Do you miss London?"

"Oh, yes, sometimes. I miss the theater and symphony. However, my parish wasn't always the easiest. I was in a high-crime area, one of those parts of London that's gentrifying but still had plenty of problems."

Problems? My sleuthing nose began to twitch. "What kind of problems?"

"Addictions, mostly. Alcohol, drugs, gambling, all of which lead to crime, poverty, violence. It's a vicious circle, but if it can be broken, lives can begin anew." As he spoke, I saw the gray pallor begin to lighten. He sounded genuinely enthusiastic. Why, then, had he left work he obviously loved?

Then we were being called to the terrace, and I didn't have an opportunity to ask more. It was time for the speeches.

Wellesley waited until we were all standing around the terrace. It was still warm, and I could smell the late summer roses, the grass that had recently been mowed, and someone's perfume. Waiters went around with glasses of champagne and sparkling water.

Me? I went straight for the champagne.

I felt the shifts of feeling, like a breeze that rustles the leaves, but it was an emotional rustle. None of us were ready for celebratory speeches, but this was still Charlie and Alice's wedding. What to do? I looked over at the happy couple, and they didn't look as happy as they should have. Still, I could see that they were sad together. There was a closeness about them that was touching.

Wellesley waited until we all had our drinks and then said, "Alistair was Charlie's best man. Not me. He asked me to stand in for him. He even gave me the speech he wrote." Wellesley waved a couple of printed sheets of paper in the air so we could all see them. "Trust me, it's a brilliant speech, full of witty anecdotes and a few jabs at Charlie. I would love to have read it to you while we were all full of good humor and the kind of happiness that a wedding brings. I would have loved, even more, to have heard Alistair read it. He assured me, as he did Alice and Charlie, that he wants the celebration to continue as planned."

He sighed and shook his head. "But a man died today." Before our eyes, he tore the speech in two. It was shocking to watch and another reminder that this wedding was like none I'd ever attended.

Wellesley put the torn pieces of paper into his suit pocket. Then he looked at the wedding couple. "Don't worry, Alistair has a copy on his hard drive. One day, he'll give that speech, maybe on your fiftieth wedding anniversary. But not today. Because today a man died. He was a lovely man. Rupert Grendell-Smythe loved life. He loved a party, and he genuinely loved Charlie. He loved him so much that he was always giving him tips on which horse to back. Rupert took a keen interest in horse racing. He'd never give me any tips, only Charlie. That's how we knew he was special."

Charlie called out, "Yes, but those horses never won. They always bobbled long before they hit the finish line."

There were a few chuckles. "I truly believe Rupert is with us at this moment, looking down, wishing he could have a glass of this lovely champagne. And what I think Rupert would want me to say to Alice and Charlie is that life is short. And, as Rupert would no doubt add, you never know how short."

Someone, somewhere clapped, but no one joined in, and it stopped as abruptly as it had started.

"You two have been lucky enough to find the person who makes you a couple. Who makes the two halves whole. Rupert had that kind of marriage, and when his wife, Lydia, died, he was lost. Now he's with her again, and for that, at least, we must be happy.

"What Rupert and Lydia taught all of us who knew them is that marriage is a true partnership. It's about sharing. This is awkward for all of us, but it's still Alice and Charlie's wedding. I'm going to suggest we offer one minute of silence to Rupert, a man who welcomed all of us to his dinner table and was so thrilled to see one of his adopted sons marry such a lovely woman."

As we stood there on the terrace in silence, I held on to the image of those brand-new shoes worn by the man who'd come to Charlie and Alice's wedding, so looking forward to a wonderful day of celebration. He'd held Alice back to congratulate her on her wedding day. Perhaps if he hadn't been so anxious to give her his good wishes, he might be here with us now. And if Charlie hadn't hustled his bride away, Alice might not.

During that minute of silence, I contemplated the quirks of fate and how just a minute or even a few seconds can make the difference between life and death, and who can ever know ahead of time how things will turn out?

It was touching and beautiful when, after a minute, one of the musicians played the First Call. And then Wellesley continued, "And now, Rupert, we wish you Godspeed."

There was a pause, and I thought Wellesley was doing an incredible job of letting us mourn Rupert and still honor Alice and Charlie.

"Lydia and Rupert modeled the kind of marriage we all wish for you, Alice and Charlie. It was one of mutual respect, of bringing up their children to be good people and of welcoming friends and neighbors like family. Lydia's kitchen always smelled like baking, and she was always happy to set an extra plate at the table.

"Alice and Charlie, you've already shown us what an incredible couple you are, and I've already seen firsthand your kindness and hospitality here in Oxford. I've rarely seen a couple I believe in more. May you live a long and happy life together, and may your marriage prosper. Ladies and gentlemen, I give you Alice and Charlie."

And we all raised our glasses and toasted the bride and groom. As I sipped the excellent champagne, I wondered if there was someone drinking champagne even now who knew perfectly well that it wasn't fate who had killed Rupert.

CHAPTER 11

he Watt sisters had taken an almost unheard of day off together to attend the wedding, leaving their hired help in charge. Their kind faces were creased with worry as they walked up to me. "What a dreadful thing to happen. Poor Charlie and Alice," Mary Watt said.

"Still," Florence added, "Look at how close they are. If they can withstand this tragedy together, they can do anything."

"And wasn't Wellesley's speech amazing?" I asked, knowing how fond they were of the stand-in best man.

"Oh, he's a treasure, and so was Rafe, to offer his lovely home for the ceremony." Florence helped herself to a tiny quiche on the tray of appetizers offered to us.

"The food's very good, too," Mary said, helping herself. "I'm almost tempted to find out who catered this affair and see if they'd like to come and work for us."

I laughed. "William is the genius behind this feast, and he runs Rafe's household. I doubt you could pry him away."

"Oh, goodness, no. And one wouldn't like to take anything from Rafe. He's such a lovely man."

The lovely man in question came up at that moment and said hello to Florence and Mary and asked them how they were faring. "Oh, well, it's a dreadful thing to witness a death, but we must also celebrate life. Alice and Charlie have had their marriage begin on a sour note, but one can only believe that it will all be sweeter from now on."

"There's William now," I said, seeing him walk past, checking that everything was as perfect as it could be, given the circumstances.

Mary said, "I'll go and congratulate him on this excellent spread." She looked at me with a twinkle in her eye. "And perhaps he'll share his recipe for those wonderful quiches. Perhaps we could experiment with some new flavors in Elderflower."

Anything that encouraged them to expand their menu sounded good to me, since I ate there quite often, being right next door.

As they went off to speak to William, Rafe said, "How are you holding up?"

I glanced around to make certain we wouldn't be overheard, even stepping closer to the edge of the terrace so a huge flower arrangement blocked us from view. "I tried to talk to Philip Wallington, the vicar, to see if there was any reason he might have been the real target."

"And?"

I shook my head. "I didn't learn much. He left London to come here. He'd been working in a rough area of London, but he seemed to enjoy his work. Doesn't that seem like a demotion to you rather than a promotion?"

"I have no idea. Shall I ask Theodore to do some digging?"

"Yes, if he wouldn't mind."

"Theodore loves keeping his old skills alive." Theodore had been a policeman in life, long before things like CSI and forensics. He was one hundred percent old school, except for computers, but it was amazing how much he could find out doing things like talking to people and asking the right questions.

From up here, I could see people milling around in the gardens below. Not everyone had decided to come to the reception, but a gratifying number had shown up. I was happy that they were putting the upset aside and supporting Alice and Charlie.

Among those on the lawn were a couple I was surprised had come. "Look who decided to show up," I said, directing Rafe's attention to a trio below.

It was Sophie and Boris Wynter standing with Giles Brighouse. For the first time all day, Sophie Wynter's black clothing and tragic demeanor fit with the surroundings.

"If you're planning to speak to them, hold me excused. Her excess of inappropriate sentiment rather put me off her."

"Me, too. But I also want to know what she has to say for herself, given your suspicions."

I didn't beeline it for the trio but meandered my way, stopping to chat briefly to the people I knew and smile and look pleasant to those I didn't. Beatrice was back to sobbing, this time on Wellesley's shoulder, so I gave them a wide berth.

When I got to the bottom of the wide, stone terrace steps, I headed in Sophie's direction. She was talking in a low, anxious voice. Her back was to me, so she couldn't see me coming, but Giles did and he said quite loudly, talking over her, "Oh, look. Here comes Lucy." Sophie immediately stopped talking. I wanted very much to hear what Sophie Wynter had been saying to her brother and their friend and why she was so anxious I shouldn't hear any of it.

She turned and glared at me as though I had no business being in Rafe's garden. I wanted to tell her that I had a lot more right to be there than she did. At least I was celebrating Charlie and Alice's wedding. At least I wished them happy.

"How are you holding up?" Boris asked in his bluff way. "I hear you were right in the thick of it."

I shook my head. "It was such a terrible shock."

I'd probably uttered the word "shock" more often in the past two hours than I had my entire life.

He nodded. "Yes. Dreadful thing."

"Worse for Alice, though. She was nearly killed." I looked directly at Sophie. "You were lucky. You missed all the drama. I think you left the church before the ceremony ended." I let my words trail up in an interrogative way. I thought for a moment she might deny walking out during the wedding vows, but, obviously knowing I must have seen her leave, she sighed. "If you must know, I couldn't face it." In a low, angry tone, as though she couldn't keep the words back, she cried, "She's not meant to be with him."

If Rafe could see her deadly earnest, he might believe, as I did, that Sophie was the most likely murderer and that she'd missed her target.

"Steady on," Giles said in a warning tone, and I wondered if he had suspicions about his old friend, too.

"Why shouldn't I speak about it? It's true."

"We're all a bit unnerved by what happened. We all grew

up together, you see. We were great friends with Alistair and Rupert." He shook his head. "Poor Charlie."

In contrast to Giles's very dapper appearance, Boris's suit looked like he'd dragged it from the back of his closet. And where Giles's shoes shone with a fresh polishing, his were covered with dust and grime.

"I don't know how they can stand it," Boris said, motioning his head to where Charlie and Alice were doing the rounds.

They did it because they had class, I wanted to explain to him. But I thought it would be like explaining advanced geometry to a turkey.

And speaking of fowl, I spied Henri standing on a wall in the garden, staring in at the party. The peacock looked like a wedding ornament perched there, his plumage glowing in the fading light of late afternoon. I excused myself and slipped away to feed him a bit of beef I'd scoffed. Henri was very partial to beef. His tail feathers rested on the wall as though his finery was dragging him down.

"I know how you feel. These fancy shoes are killing me."

The bridal couple found time to speak with everyone, and I could see the strain in Alice's eyes when they came to me, where I was still standing with Henri. "Thank you so much for all your help today," she began, looking like a woman who'd barely escaped death and now had to pretend everything was fine.

The chamber orchestra had been informed of the tragedy and had modified their selections. Even so, the music was beautiful and as suitable for a wedding reception as a wake. And in a way, that's what this was turning out to be, some strange hybrid of both.

I stopped Alice with a hand on hers. "Alice, drop the act. This is me, Lucy. I don't know how you're still on your feet." Even Henri looked interested in Alice's predicament.

She gave me a grateful smile. "I've never felt like such a fraud in all my life."

"This should be the happiest day of your life," I said, feeling my heart break for her.

She bit her lip and glanced around to make sure no one could hear us. "That's why I feel so terrible. I'm devastated about what happened to poor Rupert Grendell-Smythe, of course, but Lucy, this *is* the happiest day of my life."

I didn't know what to say, but I saw Charlie's face, and the way he smiled at her said it all. "I'm so glad you said that, because it's mine, too."

And I knew in that moment, whatever happened, these two were going to be okay.

I didn't know how to tell them about my suspicions, that Alice might have been the intended target, so I said, "You are so lucky to have found each other. Make sure you look after each other. Especially now."

CHAPTER 12

*a*s terrible as a murder at my friends' wedding was, we all had to resume our lives. I was worried about Alice and thought of little but the murder and hoped the police were on their way to discovering who'd killed Rupert. However, I still had a business to run, so I worried in between customers.

When Margaret Twigg walked into my shop, my heart sank. Margaret Twigg was the head of our coven and a very powerful witch. She was a sometime mentor to me, but her leadership always came with a price. I didn't like her much and was a bit frightened of her. She'd once demanded my cat in payment for a service she'd rendered me, though after Nyx gave her a nasty case of boils, she stopped trying to steal my familiar. Still, I respected her power and, according to Violet, she kept helping me because I was also a powerful witch. My problem was that I couldn't control my power. It was like driving down the Autobahn in a very fast car without ever having had driving lessons.

Margaret guided me, not as a favor, but to help me learn

to control my power and use it wisely. It was safer for all of us that way.

Margaret Twigg was not a knitter. She did not crochet or do any handcrafts that I was aware of. Which meant her being in my shop was going to involve her making me learn or do something I was pretty sure I'd hate.

When my great-aunt, Lavinia, came in behind her, I was positive I was right. Lavinia was my grandmother's sister and the grandmother of Violet, my shop assistant. "Lucy," Aunt Lavinia said in a slightly gushing tone. "What a lovely sweater."

"Thank you. Gran made it for me." I thought it was lovely, too, an extra-long cardigan that hung to my knees. Gran had knit it in blues and greens using a bobble stitch in some of the stripes, which gave it added texture and visual interest.

These three were the only non-vampires who knew that my grandmother, on her deathbed, had been turned into a vampire. She'd lost most of her witch powers but gained vampire powers. At least she still remembered enough about being a witch that she could offer help and advice, but for direct training, I needed the help of the twisted sisters, as I'd begun calling them.

There was only one customer in the shop, browsing, a regular who never left without buying something. But when Margaret Twigg looked at her and motioned with her hand, the woman suddenly jerked up, put back the magazine I was sure she'd been about to buy and muttered something about leaving the stove on. Then she rushed out.

"Really, Margaret," I said, exasperated. "Do you have to drive away my customers?"

"I foresee that dark forces are coming. You must be ready.

Hiding away in a knitting shop won't save you. You must learn to hone your talents. For all our sakes."

She was always disparaging of me, my shop and my lack of control, but I'd never seen her so serious before. Instinctively, I glanced at Lavinia and Violet, but they both nodded, looking grave.

"Dark forces?" I did not like the sound of that. Once I'd tangled with a soul-sucking demon, and I definitely preferred villains of the human variety.

She clucked her tongue in irritation. "Lucy, you really must keep up. If you came to more meetings of the coven or read the news bulletins, you might not live in a state of perpetual ignorance."

Ouch. I supposed she was right, though. It was bad enough reading human news of wars, politics, disasters and deaths. I didn't want to read about it in witch circles, too, so I tended to ignore the newsletters and the bulletins from the British Witches' Council. The council set out rules we all had to follow and had the power and authority to punish witches who disobeyed their decrees. Margaret Twigg was very pally with the council, and I was certain she planned to run for one of the seats herself in a future election.

She'd love lording it over all of us and being able to hand out punishments like Halloween candy.

"There's a coven of dark witches from east of the Caucasus mountains. They're trying to undermine our way of life. At the moment, they're putting faulty spells on the internet, creating bogus social media accounts to teach beginning witches bad practices, but I fear they have larger goals in mind. They want to take over the council so they'll have power over us."

I knew there were British witches lobbying to break away from the European Union of Witches (EUW) in a movement known as Wrexit. Was this just a fear-mongering campaign speech from someone who wanted my vote when council elections came around in the spring? But my instincts told me she was telling the truth. "What do you want me to do?"

"You have real power, but you're all over the place. You're vulnerable. A perfect target for a dark witch who has control over their power. They could enthrall you and make you do their bidding."

"That sounds like my last boyfriend."

"This isn't a joking matter, but that's exactly how they'll likely get to you. Beware of charming men."

"Oh, great. Now I don't just have to watch out for the creeps and cheaters," both of which I'd dated in the past, "but the nice guys as well? Might as well join a nunnery."

"They wouldn't take you," she snapped. "Now, put away your attitude and prepare to get to work. We've got to get you into shape, and there isn't much time."

That sounded like one of those intense thirty-day extreme exercise programs that I'd never got past day three on. But Margaret didn't appreciate my sarcasm, so I kept that thought to myself.

Margaret Twigg pointed to the old whisk broom that had stood in the corner of Cardinal Woolsey's long before I inherited it. "Bring your broom and meet us at my cottage tonight after dark. There will be a full moon. Perfect for your first lesson."

Somehow I didn't think I was going to learn better sweeping and housework techniques. I eyed the broom. It was so old, it looked like it might break if a squirrel tried to sit on it. How was it going to take my weight?

Was she having me on? I turned back to Margaret, but she really wasn't the joking type. "Are you suggesting what I think you're suggesting?" I couldn't even say the words. It was too ridiculous.

"Learning to fly? Of course I am."

"Great, maybe I can join the Oxford Quidditch team." There really was such a thing. I'd seen them play at University Parks, though they played an earthbound version, and I'd yet to see a real witch among them.

Margaret sniffed and turned to leave. "We'll see you tonight."

As she headed out of my shop, I called out, "And you couldn't have sent me an email?"

She turned back, a gleam of triumph in her eye. "I would, but you have a bad habit of ignoring emails you don't want to read."

Okay, she had me there.

After they left, Nyx, who never came near Margaret Twigg since the cat-napping incident, cautiously climbed down from her favorite spot in the front window.

She walked straight to the broom and pawed the straw bottom of it. I glanced at her and then at the broom. "Seriously?" I threw my hands in the air and repeated, louder and more hysterically, "Seriously?"

IT IS impossible to describe how foolish I felt turning up at

Margaret Twigg's cottage at ten o'clock that night with an old straw broom. I wore the oldest pair of jeans I could find and an ancient sweatshirt, since I suspected my butt would be in contact with the earth a few times. It was a pretty cold night, so I also brought a down jacket, gloves and a woolen hat.

I wore sneakers in case there was running involved. With my luck, my broom would take off without me and I'd spend the evening chasing it like a runaway horse.

I had my hair tied back off my face so it wouldn't get in the way. I'd searched my Grimoire for hints on broom flight but hadn't found anything at all. I still wasn't convinced this whole thing wasn't an elaborate prank. Maybe our whole coven was even now hidden behind rocks and trees waiting to jump out and laugh at me for being so naïve.

Frankly, I hoped so.

However, when I rang the bell, Margaret answered the door also dressed for the cold. She wore high leather boots, black leggings and a thick black sweater. She looked me over and nodded and let me in. She glanced behind me. "Where's your familiar?"

Nyx and I had pretty much had our first fight when I'd tried to leave her behind this evening. She'd meowed and howled even as I'd tried to explain that I didn't want Margaret Twigg to take her prisoner again; that's why I wasn't taking her.

Nyx wasn't having any of it. I finally locked her in the upstairs flat and ran downstairs, picking up the broom on my way out of the shop. When I reached the bright red car parked behind my home, I noticed a black cat-shaped shadow on the hood of the car.

Needless to say, I lost my first fight with Nyx. "She's in the car," I admitted. She'd hissed at me when I'd shut the door on her, but I wanted to keep her safe from Margaret's predatory hands.

"You'll have to fetch her."

I narrowed my gaze. I might be scared of Margaret Twigg, but my concern for my cat outweighed my fear. Mostly. "Are you going to try and keep her?" I was going to say "steal" but changed the verb at the last second.

"I wouldn't give that feral monster houseroom," she said, her eyes going glacial at the memory of what Nyx had put her through. I'd seen people allergic to cats before, but where Nyx had scratched her, she'd broken out in the most hideous boils and warts. When she'd returned the cat to its rightful owner—me—the skin condition had magically been cured. Magically being the operative word.

"Fine. We'll meet you out back."

"Leave your gloves in the car," was her final command.

Margaret picked up a long whip. I eyed it dubiously, wondering who—or what—she was planning to use it on.

I could see Nyx's golden eyes glowing as I grew near the car. No doubt she could get out of a locked car if she wanted to badly enough, but I liked to think she respected me, at least a little, and let me think I was the boss.

I opened the door, and after shooting me an expression that was a cat's version of *I told you so,* she jumped down onto the gravel path and walked ahead of me. Me, my black cat and my broom. We were a walking cliché. All I needed was a pointy hat and a wart on my nose.

We went around the side of the stone cottage and through an iron gate that led into a garden where Margaret Twigg grew medicinal herbs and plants. It was thriving, even in late autumn. Green thumb or magic? With Margaret Twigg, you never knew.

Nyx's ears twitched when she heard rustling coming from the garden to her left, but she didn't give in to temptation. Instead, she remained resolutely by my side. She had a way of communicating with me where I had the sensation of experiencing words in my head, not as though I'd heard them but as if they were placed in my head. It was hard to explain. Anyway, the words in my head were *stay calm*. Which was easier thought than done. I could feel the jangle of nerves and my increased heart rate. I didn't much care for flying in planes, so I really wasn't thrilled at the idea of climbing onto cleaning supplies and attempting to take flight.

The moon didn't help. It might be full, but that only made silvery shadows of the shrubbery. What was left of the ancient forest of Wychwood looked to my nervous eyes like ancient creatures ready to advance on me.

Fortunately, when Margaret emerged from her cottage, now in a heavy wool coat and still carrying that whip, Aunt Lavinia and Violet came out with her. Aunt Lavinia, also probably sensing how nervous I felt, walked forward and said, "Welcome, Lucy." She put her gloved hands on my upper arms. "Blessed be."

Violet just said, "Hi, Lucy. I hope you learn fast. It's freezing out here."

The utter normality of that, strangely, calmed me down more than anything. I fell into step with my cousin. "Can you fly a broom?" I had to ask.

"Of course. It's one of the first things we learn. Not that we use it much, obviously. In the old days, they didn't have to contend with air traffic, drones and shift workers. Besides, nowadays, it's much easier to drive or fly conventionally. The broom is only a good skill. You might need to use it in a pinch."

"Then why is she making me learn?" I jerked my broom handle toward Margaret.

"She's convinced that you need to learn everything you should have when you were a young witch. Since your mother refused to accept your magic, never mind her own, you never got any training." She turned to me, and even in the near dark, I could see that she looked serious. "Remember how your mother nearly died? She made herself vulnerable by denying her own powers."

I nodded. It wasn't like I'd ever forget how that soul-sucking demon very nearly killed my mom. "I don't want that to happen to me."

"Then be a good sport. You'll learn to fly your broom and probably never need to do it again."

"Like getting my learner's permit and never bothering to pass the driving test."

"Something like that."

I felt better if no one was going to expect me to whisk around on a broom. I groaned at my own bad pun. I made myself feel better on the rest of the short walk by thinking of even worse ones. I'd sweep into a room. Get a handle on directions. Bristle if anyone criticized my driving... They were bad. But I was nervous.

We entered a large clearing surrounded by trees. I wasn't sure whether we were still on Margaret Twigg's land or in the forest, but it was definitely private. Whatever happened, no one from the outside would be able to see us. That was a bonus.

Nyx went ahead and then turned, her eyes glowing gold in the moonlight. I took a deep breath and reminded myself that I didn't have to do anything I didn't want to. I noticed tingling in my fingers and realized it was the hand that was wrapped around the broom. Without gloves, my naked palm came into contact with the old wood. Either I'd been squeezing it so tight I was getting pins and needles, or something very strange was happening. Given my company, who I was and where I was, I suspected the latter.

Still, I'd come here to learn, hadn't I? I gathered my courage and walked forward to where the three witches and my familiar now waited. The closer I drew, the more my hand began to tingle. There was no doubt in my mind now that this was no joke. My broom was indeed magic. The question was, was I magic enough to fly it?

Margaret Twigg looked at me in her usual condescending way. "Lucy. Stop looking so frightened. It's not much different than learning to ride a horse."

I'd never been much of a horse rider. In fact, I vividly remembered trail riding at summer camp when the ranch hand hadn't fastened the saddle on properly and when I tried to mount, the saddle slipped all the way under my horse's belly with me still attached.

"The wood in that broom came from here, you know. From this ancient forest." She raised her hands as though thanking the forest for the wood. "That's why we'll train you here. This is where your broom began life as a young tree."

Well, that was kind of cool. I was going to ask her how long ago that was, but I really didn't want to know. But then I remembered what had happened to that ancient beam in the church, and I had to ask. "Is it very old?"

Margaret shrugged. "That depends on your definition of old. A couple of hundred years, I should think."

Yes, that neatly encompassed my definition of old. Especially if we were talking about something that was going to take me up off the ground. Now I was even more nervous. "It's not full of deathwatch beetle, is it?"

"Of course not. Stop being so foolish. This is a skill you should have learned years ago."

"I really don't know if I'm cut out for this. I don't have very good balance." I kept picturing myself tumbling onto the hard ground. Possibly from a very great height.

"Your grandmother used this broom very comfortably, and her mother before her. It is part of your craft. It's part of you."

The thought of my grandmother zooming around at night was almost as disconcerting as knowing that even now she was beginning her nightly escapades as a vampire.

Well, I might as well get this over with. "All right. What do I do first?"

"First, we have a demonstration."

If that meant I didn't have to be on the broom, I was all for a demonstration.

I tried to hand Margaret my flying broom, but she held her hands up and stepped back.

I was puzzled. "Aren't you going to demonstrate it?"

She shook her head so hard, those crazy curls bounced like metal bedsprings that had been struck by lightning. "Absolutely not. No witch should ever ride another's broom unless it's been passed to her, as yours was to you down your family line. A broom is made specially for each witch."

Aunt Lavinia echoed the sentiment. "The same broom makers have done them for all our family. One day, you'll have a special broom made for your daughter."

I didn't know many things, but one thing I was sure of. I was never going to let any kid of mine ride a broom.

CHAPTER 13

"Okay." I looked around. "Then who's going to demonstrate?"

Three pairs of witch eyes turned to my cat, who was still sitting in the middle of the circle, her golden eyes glowing. "Nyx?" I thought that was a terrible idea. I didn't know how many lives Nyx had started with when I first met her, but she had to have used a few of them by now. I did not want to lose my cat.

However, at the sound of her name, my familiar rose and stepped forward.

Margaret Twigg was almost as horrified at the thought of touching my cat as she was of touching my family's broom. Standing well out of scratching distance, she said, "Now, settle the bristles so they just touch the earth and angle the handle towards the moon."

That wasn't very hard. The moon was full, so it was pretty easy to aim at.

As soon as I had it set up, Nyx daintily walked up the

broom like a gymnast on the balance beam. Very impressive. She didn't even wobble.

"Now we set the direction."

"You mean like a GPS?"

Margaret chuckled, which always sounded like an evil cackle to me. "Not exactly. But if that helps you visualize the process, then fine."

What I was visualizing right now was being back in my bed all snuggled up with a pillow over my head to block out light and noise.

I was puzzled. "But Nyx has never been on the broom before."

She gave her superior smirk. And no one could smirk in a more superior fashion than Margaret Twigg. "Your cat is also from a long line of familiars connected with your family."

Okay then. Nyx gave me a look that was slightly piteous. I supposed I should have figured that out by now.

"The rest is as simple as a spell. Mostly all you're doing is focusing your intention. Concentrate. Picture the broom riding around this thicket. Trying to rhyme helps you bring focus."

I felt a bit foolish making up an impromptu rhyme in front of these much more experienced witches, but they were all looking at me and standing there in expectant silence. I closed my eyes. As I pictured the broom circling the clearing, I felt my hand begin to tingle again. Instinctively, I reached up my index finger as I traced a circle around the edge of the clearing. I said, more as though I was reciting a rhyme I already knew than making up a fresh one, "Dear Broom, I call to thee. Travel in a circle from tree to tree. When you are done, return to me. So I will, so mote it be."

Then I gave a gasp as I felt a spurt of energy. The broom jerked out my hand. My eyes opened wide in time to see the broom launch into the air like a rocket. Nyx braced herself, and I was certain her claws were digging into the wood. Her ears pressed back, but to my shock and amazement, the broom followed my instructions. It took a perfectly nice circle around the edge of the clearing and then landed back in exactly the position it started from.

Nyx turned to look at me over her shoulder, not even jumping off the broom. It was as though she said, "Come on in, the water's fine."

Aunt Lavinia clapped her hands. "Well done, Lucy. That's excellent for a first attempt."

Violet nodded. "Now you try, Lucy."

There was a certain smug anticipation in her tone. Violet and I had become good friends, but there was still an edge of competition between us. I seemed to have more raw power than she did, but she was much more practiced in our craft. I had a notion she was looking forward to watching me tumble. And that would make one of us.

Still, if there was something bad coming our way, I supposed I owed it to my fellow witches to at least learn the rudimentary skills. I promised myself I was not going to make a habit of flying on brooms.

I eyed Margaret Twigg. "What's the whip for?"

"Should the broom get away from you, I'd be able to retrieve it."

The whip wasn't very long. "But only at the very beginning?"

"Yes. After that, you're on your own."

I wished I hadn't asked.

"Now. You can begin with a standing start, as it is right now, or a floating start, when the broom is suspended in the air and you mount it like a bicycle."

I looked at the old broom. "Which one is the easiest?"

Margaret Twigg threw her hands up in the air, and the whip twitched as though it really wanted to smack me. "Never mind what's easiest. You'll try both."

Since the broom was already in the ground position, I decided to start with that. I went forward and stepped one leg over the broom. I repeated the same verse as before since it had worked so well and hoped that we would both return safely.

Margaret told me to lean forward and clasp the broom handle with both hands. I did and then I felt that same surge of energy, and the broom came up off the ground so quickly, it whacked me on the hipbone. "Ow," I cried just as Nyx and I took off with a lurch.

I can't describe the feeling of flying on a broom. It was a little bit like riding a bike, with the feeling of wind in my face and the narrow perch. But when I looked down, I didn't think of riding a bike anymore.

The earth seemed a long way below. The three witches were following my progress, their faces pale in the moonlight. I wanted to enjoy this moment, but I was actually terrified. I mean, I was sitting on a broom about thirty feet above the ground. What if the broom decided it didn't want to fly anymore, or I lost concentration, which was probably the same thing as running out of gas? So instead of daydreaming and looking all around, I focused all my attention on the circle we were making. Nyx seemed pretty relaxed, and it was amazing skimming above the treetops. Something whizzed past, and I realized it was a bat.

Our circle completed, we began to descend. We landed with a bump, but at least we landed. I dismounted, feeling wobbly in my knees. I'd been so focused on trying to stay aloft that I hadn't really thought about the fact that I, a grown woman, had somehow managed to balance on the handle of a broom. In the air. With my cat.

Lavinia and Violet both clapped. Margaret Twigg did not.

"Now," she said, "you'll practice mounting the broom while it's aloft."

I thought it might have been nice if she'd given me a chance to catch my breath and let my legs stop shaking, but Margaret Twigg wasn't one for worrying about other people's feelings. Especially if those feelings happened to be mine.

Nyx was still on the broom, and she looked to me expectantly. She clearly knew what came next, even if I didn't.

Margaret instructed me to picture the broom sitting in the air at the right height for me to mount it. I pictured something about bicycle seat height, and then with my tingling right hand, I simply lifted the back end of the broom without touching it. Surprisingly, it worked. I was a bit more nervous getting on this way. But at least the broom didn't come up and whack me in the hip this time. Still, there was something very disconcerting about positioning myself on a broom while it hovered in midair. How could I not fall off? How could I not end up as I had that day on the horse, climbing on all right and then finding myself sliding underneath until I was upside down? I had no idea. Those physics were beyond me. But the good news was that I managed to mount without any problem at all. I had to resist the urge to wrap my arms around Nyx as though she were my boyfriend and we were riding a motorcycle down a twisty road.

If Margaret Twigg hadn't been watching me, I might've done it, but there was something about having that sharp critical gaze on me that made me concentrate for all I was worth. Once more, Nyx and I did a circle around the clearing. I was feeling pretty confident when we returned. If there was a witches' driver's test, I thought I should get a gold star. But of course, when Margaret Twigg was involved, she wasn't satisfied unless I was experiencing one of the following: terror, complete lack of self-esteem, feeling foolish. If she got me feeling all three of those things at the same time, she gave herself a gold star.

Even as Great-Aunt Lavinia was congratulating me and telling me that I was a natural, Margaret Twigg was saying, "All right. I want you to ride to my cottage, pick a sprig of rosemary from my garden and bring it back."

I felt my eyes grow wide. Even Nyx twitched her tail as though she thought Margaret was pushing it. And since Nyx was my copilot, I didn't think she wanted me pushed out of my comfort zone too quickly, either. "What?"

"You can do it. I'll expect you back here in five minutes."

Oh, good, just to add to my stress, now I had a time limit on top of the larger task of flying a broom. I wanted to argue, but there was something about Margaret that made it very difficult for me to engage in conflict with her. Instead, I blew out a huge breath the way I used to when my mom criticized my grades in high school and then stomped over to the broom. I moved my hand up so quickly that the broom bounced, and Nyx let out a surprised meow.

"Sorry, Nyx," I said, feeling terrible. I shouldn't take my

temper out on my poor familiar. It was Margaret Twigg I wanted to let out a startled meow at.

The way Margaret's cat eyes were looking at me, I suspected she could read my mind. Good.

I mounted the broom. Aunt Lavinia came up to me and touched my shoulder. "Take your time, Lucy. Focus. Concentrate. You can do it. Nyx is there to help you."

I was so happy I had someone here who actually seemed to care about me. I nodded and breathed in and out, slowly regaining my focus. I pictured Margaret's cottage and the lush herb garden I'd walked through. I was sorely tempted to make a rude rhyme and thought of all the satisfying things that would rhyme with Twigg, but the reality was I wanted to survive this night more. I said, "Dear Broom, please take me to Margaret Twigg's home, to a clump of rosemary on its own. So I will, so mote it be."

I clung to the ancient wooden handle of that broom so tightly I could feel my palms begin to sweat. But then I thought of all the other witches who'd gone before me on that very broom, including my grandmother. Without the scrutiny of the three witches, I started to feel as though I were on one of those terrible rides at the fairground, the kind that makes your stomach feel like it's flipped inside out and is wedged in your throat. But as I looked down over the trees, I suddenly felt like a kid again. This couldn't be happening, and yet it was.

I was flying.

It wasn't far to Margaret Twigg's cottage, and soon we were clearing the edge of the forest and I nudged the handle of the broom down. I wasn't sure if it needed the extra steering, but the broom responded. It brought us right down in the herb garden, and to my delight, we were on a path beside a healthy-looking rosemary bush. I snapped a largish piece of the dark green spiky herb, and the spicy fragrance of rosemary briefly filled the air. I was so delighted, I seriously wanted to go for a joyride, but I had a five-minute deadline, and I was determined I'd be back within the time limit.

I told the broom that we wanted to return, and Nyx and I sailed up again over the trees. I felt sheer joy as the breeze we were making by flying lifted the wisps of my hair that had come out of the ponytail. The air was cold and crisp, and below, the trees blocked anyone's view of us. Even when we crossed fields, they were empty, sleeping quietly.

When we returned, I presented Margaret with the sprig of rosemary as though it were a bouquet of roses. She gave a tiny smile and said, "Well done, Lucy."

Even though Lavinia and Violet had been clapping and congratulating me all night, those three words from Margaret filled me with pride.

She looked at me in a considering way and then said, "You have one more task. I want you to fly to the standing stones and bring me back the round pebble that's sitting on top of the headstone."

I was puzzled. That was pretty specific. I wrinkled my brow. "How do you know there's a round pebble on top of the headstone?"

She looked to me like I was a particularly dim student. "Because I put it there."

I did not think she'd taken a twelve-foot ladder out to the standing stones and climbed up to the headstone. She'd flown there herself.

"I won't be able to land, will I?"

That smug, borderline evil smile tilted her lips. "No. You will hover, reach out one hand and pick up the stone. Then you will circle and return here."

I thought I had been doing very well, but this was advanced driver training. "Are you sure I can handle it?"

She shook her head. "Not at all. But we'll see, won't we?"

I glanced at my two witch relatives, but they both nodded at me encouragingly.

"Okay," I said. "Here goes." I might have sounded hard done by, but I was really starting to enjoy this flying thing. I just didn't want the twisted sisters to know.

I set my internal GPS, muttered my rhyme, and off we went. This was a longer ride, and it was exhilarating. As we sailed across the A40 motorway, I looked down and saw headlights. What if someone looked up and saw us? I wondered if that ever happened. But we flew without any kind of lights. No doubt if a motorist looked up in the sky and saw what they thought was a witch flying on a broom, they'd think they'd eaten something bad. Or that it was a very big bird. They'd doubt their senses before they believed in such foolishness as flying witches. Or at least I hoped so.

The standing stones in the moonlight looked like ladies in white gauze gowns dancing. I'd been there before during a full moon, for coven events, but naturally, I'd never seen the stones from this angle. As I came closer, I experienced the feeling as though I were dancing with them. I took a couple of turns around the stones and then, feeling particularly daring, I took us between two of them where there was the widest gap. I was flying in every sense of the word.

I discovered that I could, in fact, use the broom's handle to steer us. I could tell it where to go, but I could also manually point to where I wished to go. However, I didn't want to crash right into the stone, so I needed to go close but not too close. Also, I had no idea how to pause in midair long enough to grab the pebble. We sailed past, and I could see the perfect round pebble perched in the middle, on the top of the head stone. "Nyx, what do I do? How do I put this thing on pause?"

And then the words came to me. "Broom, hover."

I said those words aloud and, like magic, we began to hover. By reaching out, I was able to scoop up the pebble.

As we rode back home, I said, "Nyx, we are a great team."

I swear she shook her head. And if I could have seen her face, I'd bet she was rolling her eyes.

When I returned back to the clearing and handed over the pebble, Margaret Twigg said, "Good. That's enough for tonight. But I want you here once a week, Lucy."

"Once a week?" It wasn't the flying lessons that I minded so much, but the thought of spending one evening every week with Margaret Twigg took a lot of the fun out of zooming through the air on a broom.

She looked quite stern. "You've a great deal to learn, and if you're not pushed, you grow lazy."

I wanted to argue, but I knew she was right. I just had so much to learn in every area of my life. Between trying to figure out how to knit and still being quite new at running a retail store, and trying to pack in a lifetime's worth of witch training, and trying to keep Alice safe and stop a murderer, I barely had any time left over. Still, if I was going to take this witch gig seriously, and she wasn't making it up about dark forces coming our way, I knew I had to sharpen my skills. So I nodded and agreed that I'd be back at the same time next week.

We all went our separate ways then, and Nyx and I drove back to Oxford. As we headed down the A40, I couldn't resist looking up in the sky to see if I could see any witches flying. I didn't see any, but I wouldn't put it past the three twisted sisters I'd just left to be careening around on their brooms for fun.

When I returned home, as I was getting out of my car, a dark and dangerous-looking man emerged from the shadows and stepped toward me. I'd have screamed except I was becoming used to the sight.

"What are you doing here?" I asked Rafe. "And why are you waiting outside?" It wasn't like he needed a key to get in.

Nyx ran to him like he was a succulent bowl of fresh tuna, and he automatically bent and scooped her up. She crawled up and over his shoulder and hung there in one of her favorite positions. "I heard about your evening's activities. I wanted to make sure you were all right."

In truth, I was happy to see him. I was bubbling over with excitement and dying to tell someone. And there were very few people in my life to whom I could safely gush about my experiences flying on a broom.

"It was amazing," I said. I opened the door, and we all went in. He followed me upstairs to my flat. I'd planned to make myself some hot cocoa, but now that Rafe was here, I asked, "Would you like a glass of red wine?" He sometimes drank wine, and it was a nice way for us to share something. He nodded and reached into the high cupboard where I kept the wine. I handed him the corkscrew and fetched two glasses.

We sat on my couch, and I told him about my evening. "It was so cool," I cried. "Nyx was amazing. Rafe, I flew."

He was looking at me indulgently. "It's a good feeling, isn't it?"

"You...?"

"Well, it's not exactly flying when we do it. It's more just moving very, very quickly."

I thought that was pretty cool too.

But I didn't think he'd come only to talk flying. "Has Theodore discovered anything about the murder?"

CHAPTER 14

"Theodore has been looking into Philip Wallington's background." Rafe shifted and crossed one elegant leg over the other. "It seems he didn't tell the police everything."

I couldn't believe it. "You're telling me an Anglican vicar lied?"

He made a back-and-forth motion with his head. "No. He didn't lie, exactly. It was more a sin of omission."

That made me feel better. "Okay. I'm listening."

"It's the reason he moved from London to this rather sleepy backwater of Moreton-under-Wychwood that's interesting."

"And the reason is?"

"His life was threatened."

Somebody wanted to kill that nice vicar? "What?"

"My reading of Philip Wallington is that he genuinely wants to do good, but perhaps he's a bit of a hothead. His ministry was in a bad part of London, one rife with drugs and gangs. He was very successful in getting people off drugs and helping with gambling and alcohol addictions. He started ambitious programs, trained volunteers, provided food and counseling, places to stay, halfway houses and jobs. He was quite successful."

"That sounds wonderful. What went wrong?"

"He was too successful. He made enemies of some very powerful people, the kind who run drugs and gambling and so on."

"I hate that there are people like that in the world."

"So, it appears, does the vicar. He was warned to stop some of his programs, but he refused."

"Oh, dear. Did something bad happen?"

"He was beaten. Not too badly, but enough that the church heeded the warning. He still argued that he wanted to stay and continue his work, but his superiors decided to take him out of harm's way."

"And so the church sent him to Moreton-under-Wychwood."

"Exactly."

Politics were everywhere it seemed, even in the church and the witches' council. We all had to abide by rules set by other people. I understood how Philip Wallington must feel, but I didn't see how his London work was relevant to what had happened at Alice and Charlie's wedding. "Wouldn't these crime lords be happy to get rid of the zealous vicar? He's gone. They've won. Why kill him?"

"Because getting rid of him permanently sends a pretty strong message to other do-gooders. You see, he's quite famous in certain circles."

"It seems wrong that someone who tries so hard to do good should be targeted by the forces of evil."

He looked at me with a quizzical expression on his face. "And yet, it happens."

I knew this was true. Still, I didn't have to like it. "So your theory is that he was followed from London by these bad dudes? And they went through this elaborate beam-crashing exercise to stop him from helping addicts?" I thought it seemed a bit far-fetched.

"Think about it. Most of the guests at this wedding were from London. It's been on national news. They could be sending a message."

"Did Theodore happen to find out whether any crime bosses or their known associates were in Moreton-Under-Wychwood on the day of the wedding?"

"He's still looking into that."

"I don't know. My money's still on Sophie Wynter. You saw her sobbing through Alice and Charlie's wedding service. And then she slipped out before it was over. She definitely had time to run around the church, sneak into the organ loft and drop that beam. And it wasn't Rupert Grendell-Smythe she was aiming for. It was Alice."

He looked unconvinced. "It's not that I don't think she would've done Alice a mischief if she could, but this crime was planned before the wedding day. Sophie Wynter doesn't seem strong enough to have sawed through that beam. She had help."

"What about that brother of hers? Boris. He's a burly, rugby-playing, thick-armed muscleman. He could have done it. And he left the church with her."

"I suppose he could. But would he really kill his sister's rival? It's taking brotherly love a bit far, don't you think?"

"I never had a brother, so I wouldn't know. It seems pretty crazy to me. But then, maybe he's as crazy as she is."

"The trouble is that there could be several people who were the real targets. It makes finding out who the murderer is a bit more challenging when we're not certain of the victim."

As I had many times since the wedding, I went over in my head who'd been near enough to that beam that they could have easily been killed. "What about Charlie's parents? They were also in the line of fire. If Charlie's mother hadn't had the lightning-quick reflexes to throw her husband out of the way and herself on top of him, they'd have been crushed too. What has Theodore discovered about them?"

"The truth is, Lucy, everyone has their secrets. No doubt, Charlie's parents have them too. So far, we haven't unearthed anything that would suggest them as targets for murder. They were friendly with Rupert Grendell-Smythe and his wife and the families of all those young men who stood up with Charlie. They all lived in or near Wembley."

I was so frustrated. First, because I was constantly plagued by low-level worry about Alice. Sophie and Boris were still staying in Oxford. I wished they would go away. That black widow spider should go back to the middle of her own web and stay away from Oxford.

I'd done my best to put a protection spell on Alice. I'd also given her a special present from me to her. It was a pretty crystal necklace of amethyst, lapis lazuli and obsidian. The stones in themselves had protective properties, but I'd ramped it up as much as I could with protective spells. The result was a powerful amulet and, fortunately, Alice was sentimental enough that she wore it all the time.

Poor Alice and Charlie. Not only had their wedding been badly marred by Rupert Grendell-Smythe's murder, but they'd decided to postpone their honeymoon as well.

The newly wedded pair should have been happily wandering the book stacks of the greatest libraries in the world but instead were still here in Oxford. I was upset when she first told me they weren't going away, as I'd believed at least they'd be safe when they were far away on their honeymoon. However, neither of them had wanted to abandon Alistair so soon after the shock and horror of losing his father like that. They weren't the kind of people to complain about their bad luck, but I knew they felt somehow responsible because the death had happened during their wedding.

And so they stayed on in Oxford. Alistair remained because the police weren't releasing his father's body yet. His job had given him compassionate leave. Sophie and Boris stayed on, and I had no idea why. They didn't seem worried about missing work. Did they even have jobs? I suspected that Sophie wanted to be near Charlie in the vain hope that in the aftermath of the tragedy, he and Alice would break up. I could've told her that wasn't going to happen, and now that Alice and Charlie had talked frankly about Sophie and Charlie's past relationship, I didn't think that Sophie was any threat to the relationship. If anything, knowing Alice's soft heart, she felt nothing but compassion for Charlie's ex, even though the woman was horrible to her.

Wellesley, Nigel and Giles had also decided to stay on.

Wellesley seemed to have assistants who could do most of his work. Giles was also in banking, but he'd managed to take holidays, and Nigel was a book editor who had told his associates he'd be working remotely.

Beatrice ended up remaining in Oxford as well. I didn't think she'd intended to, but she was the sort of person who didn't like to be left out. If everyone else from the wedding party was going to remain, so would she. She worked in social media so she could also work remotely.

Even though I was worried about Alice and Charlie, I still had a business to run. I couldn't spend all my life hovering around the newlyweds trying to keep them safe. I'd given Alice the protection amulet, and I'd enlisted Violet's help in putting a protection circle around Frogg's Books. There wasn't much more I could do, unless I could solve the murder, which, as usual, was more difficult than it appeared.

I still believed that Sophie Wynter was the one with the greatest motive to harm Alice, but I had learned from experience that I shouldn't focus on a pet theory to the exclusion of any others. Therefore, I was keenly interested in what Theodore could discover about the backgrounds of other possible suspects and other possible targets. Maybe someone other than Alice or Rupert had been the real intended target. Well, at one point, I'd believed it was me and that Rafe's beloved wife had tried to kill me.

I still felt bad about that. One of these days, I was going to take some flowers to Constance's memorial stone and apologize in person. It didn't matter if she couldn't hear me; she'd been a fellow witch, and we had Rafe in common. Even, if he was to be believed, some sort of family connection. I didn't want to be on bad terms with the first woman Rafe had ever loved, even if she was nothing but a long-departed ghost.

So I wondered about the rest of the wedding party, as well. Could one of Charlie's or Alice's friends have been the real target?

And why?

One of the things I'd discovered about murder was that the motive was rarely obvious or straightforward. Often it was a hurt or anger that had festered unexamined and unshared for years, sometimes decades. Then something made the anger, the ill will, the fear or the hatred flare up. That was another reason why I was so suspicious of Sophie Wynter. Her motive was so beautifully clear. She'd been in love with Charlie for decades; she was quite literally crazy about him. The hope that had kept her going was that one day she and Charlie would end up together.

Thanks to a fortune-teller she'd met at a charity event. One who no doubt told her what she wanted to hear. We only had Sophie's word for it that the fortune-teller had predicted she'd end up with Charlie. I wouldn't put it past Sophie to make the whole thing up.

No matter how she'd come by that notion, though, she definitely had it bad for Charlie, and that made Alice her enemy.

But it was a long way from obsession to murder. Did she hate Alice enough to kill her? Rafe was probably right that if she had dropped that beam, she hadn't done it alone.

When Violet and I found ourselves alone in the shop, we talked about the murder a lot more than we talked about new stock that I should be ordering or the classes we should be setting up for winter.

We were careful, though. The minute we heard those cheerful bells announcing a customer, we'd immediately change the subject to something knitting- or crochet-related so as not to freak out the paying customers. And so it was, that Thursday afternoon, we were in the middle of speculating about how far Sophie Wynter would really go to try and recapture Charlie's affection when the cheerful bells rang as someone came into the shop.

We stopped talking at once, and I suggested that we should change the window display to feature Halloween. The British never used to celebrate the great candy-grabbing holiday. Instead, they celebrate Guy Fawkes Night, which was a big bonfire night with hardly any dressing up.

Halloween was a lot more fun if you were a kid. And, as with so many other things, the influence of North America grew stronger every year. Now it was quite common to see little children dressed up like ghosts and goblins on October thirty-first out knocking on doors, asking for candy.

Since I was an American, I felt perfectly comfortable promoting this wonderful holiday on behalf of children everywhere. Besides, big, fat orange pumpkins, black cats and full moons made for an interesting backdrop to warm, chunky knit sweaters, gloves, hats and scarves.

At the same time, I launched loudly into ideas about the window display, Violet began talking about our next set of lessons. It must've sounded rather strange to walk in on two entirely different conversations while there were only the two of us in the shop. We both turned at the same time to see who had entered.

I think we were both surprised to discover that it wasn't a regular customer. In fact, it wasn't a customer at all who stood

there looking around rather uncertainly. It was Alistair Grendell-Smythe. We both hesitated a second too long. I was
trying to come up with the appropriate greeting, and I
suspected Violet was doing the same. Then, at the very same
moment, we both moved forward toward the man. I said,
"Alistair. What a nice surprise."

And Violet said, "Well, look what the cat dragged in."

Since Nyx had, in fact, taken advantage of him opening
the door to scoot in at the same time, there was just enough
truth in her teasing line to make us all laugh.

He seemed as though he wanted to turn around and leave
as quickly as he'd entered, and perhaps he would have if Nyx
hadn't decided he was good for some affection. Or perhaps
she felt his sadness and wanted to give him some affection.
Whatever the motive, she began to butt her head against his
ankle and rub up against his trouser leg.

"I hope you're not allergic," I said.

He shook his head. "No. I like cats." He leaned down and
scooped her up. I could tell that she liked him from the way
she immediately scaled his chest and then crawled over his
shoulder and hung there.

I usually only saw her do that with Rafe. So I could say
with confidence, "She likes you."

"Animals usually do."

We witches exchanged glances. Violet didn't seem to
know any more than I did what Rupert's son was doing here.
His red hair was all over the place, and he needed a shave.
He'd only planned to stay in Oxford a few days, and he'd
been here going on two weeks, so his clothes looked creased
and worn too many times. "You're not a knitter, are you?"

"No." He petted Nyx in long, slow, gliding strokes from

her blissed-out head to her twitching tail. By giving her all his attention, he didn't have to look at us. "I don't know what to do with myself. I'm going crazy." He looked at Violet with the shattered eyes of someone who wasn't sleeping properly. "I remembered how nice you were to me at the wedding. After. I mean, when it happened."

She took a step closer to him. "Of course."

"I was wondering if maybe I could take you for lunch or tea. I just want someone to talk to."

It was eleven-thirty in the morning. Too late for coffee and too early for lunch, but Violet didn't have set break times, and she tended to do what she pleased. She said, "Actually, I'm very hungry. Lunch would be wonderful." She looked at me. "You don't mind, do you, Lucy?"

I was way too pleased to think she might ease Alistair's grief. "Go ahead. I was only going to start working on the window display anyway. I can do that and take care of any customers we have. Have a nice lunch."

She went to fetch her purse. I asked Alistair, "How are you doing?"

He shook his head and opened his mouth as though searching for the right words. "It's like I've been kicked. I took a soccer ball to the solar plexus once. That's what this reminds me of. I wake up and I wonder what this terrible pain is and then I remember."

There wasn't much I could do for him, but I could help him sleep. After seeing the success of Violet's energy tea, I'd been practicing making my own selection of medicinal teas. There were plenty of recipes in my Grimoire. I modified one, tweaking a little valerian root here and chamomile flowers there. It was wonderful for helping a person drift off to sleep and helping them get back to sleep when they woke in the middle of the night. I knew, since I'd been practicing on myself. Alistair wasn't the only one who woke in the night still traumatized by what we'd witnessed at the wedding. I suspected that if I took my own sadness and multiplied it by a thousand, I might come close to what this recently orphaned son was feeling.

"I've got some nice calming herbal tea. I'll send you home with some. Make sure you have a cup before you go to bed. It will help you sleep, I promise."

I wanted to offer him my washing machine, but maybe that was too familiar. No doubt his hotel had some kind of service and it hadn't occurred to him to use it. Laundry probably wasn't high on his priority list.

"I'd be truly grateful."

When Violet returned with her purse, I could see that she'd also taken the time to comb her hair and freshen her makeup. Alistair said, "I know it's only next door, but do you mind if we go to the Miss Watts? They're so comfortable, and I've known them for such a long time."

I watched them leave, and as I did, I sensed a closeness there that was more than just someone who was grieving wanting to talk to someone who was a good listener. Out of this terrible tragedy, I wondered if love might bloom. I just hoped Violet would have the sense to take things really slowly. Alistair wasn't in the best emotional condition to begin a new relationship, and Violet tended to rush things.

As they left, I had another thought. The Miss Watts had served those boys tea and breakfast when they'd been undergrads at Cardinal College. Why hadn't I thought to ask the ladies next door what they knew? They'd been around a long time, and I suspected they knew quite a bit about the men who'd made up Charlie's wedding team.

I decided to pop next door myself today and subtly question the Watt sisters. I couldn't believe I hadn't thought of it before. I'd be seriously concerned that I was letting my client down if anyone ever actually paid me to be a detective.

CHAPTER 15

*W*hen I walked into Elderflower Tea Shop later that afternoon, I realized I wasn't just here to be nosy about Charlie and his friends when they'd been undergrads. I needed good company and the sustenance that only a proper English afternoon tea can give a person. I needed scones and clotted cream and the Watt sisters' homemade strawberry jam, along with a pot of strong English tea served in a flower-patterned teacup. I was having my second lesson in broom flying that evening. I needed the sustenance and the good cheer.

The Miss Watts might not fuss over me quite as enthusiastically as they did over Wellesley and his friends, but I still received a flattering amount of attention. They were like honorary great-aunts to me, Florence and Mary Watt. They'd been very good friends of my grandmother's, and I had helped them when a murder was committed in this very shop. So it was perfectly natural for me to suggest that they sit down and join me in a cup of tea. I'd chosen my time carefully, when I knew it wouldn't be too busy. The three of us sat down together, though Mary Watt made sure her seat was facing the entrance to the restaurant so she could jump up if any customers should arrive.

They had a kitchen helper, they told me, a young woman from Paris. Mary, who was in charge of the kitchen and prided herself on serving the best scones in all of England, said, "Lisette is a very nice girl. She trained at the Cordon Bleu."

"Wow." I glanced at the blackboard, hoping to find a few French-inspired meals, but the menu remained the same as always. The most French-sounding thing on it was quiche Lorraine.

"I'm sure she's very good with snails and frogs' legs," Mary said, her lack of interest in ever tasting either of those dishes being evident in her tone. "But they don't teach them much in the way of scones at the Cordon Bleu. Still, bless her, she's very willing to learn. And I have high hopes that she will improve." She shook her head. "I just wish she wouldn't keep trying to push new menu items at us. Tourists come here for good British standbys. They don't want foreign food. They can go to the continent if they want that."

I sincerely felt for that poor young woman in the kitchen trying to bring some Cordon Bleu flair into the Miss Watts' lives. My stomach hoped she'd prevail, but my common sense suggested I should be grateful that Miss Watt's scones were so good.

As I reached for one, Mary leaned forward and said softly, "Don't you worry, dear. I baked the scones that we'll be eating. Lisette's getting better by the day, but she hasn't quite got my touch. Not yet."

Because I loved these two old ladies, I loyally said that I

couldn't imagine anyone ever making scones quite as delicious as those made by Mary Watt. It wasn't just loyalty. It was actually true. What I didn't say was that there was more to life than scones. Though not, perhaps, at teatime.

So I took a scone with pleasure, breaking open the golden treat, still warm from the oven. There was an argument between the people of Devon and the people of Cornwall about which way a person should eat a scone. One of them, and I could never remember which, insisted that jam had to go on first with the cream on top, while their rivals said exactly the opposite.

While this might suggest that the people of Cornwall and Devon didn't have enough to do, I remained impartial by putting jam first and then cream on one side of my scone and cream first and then jam on the other side. I'd never noticed that it made much difference to the flavor, but now it had become a habit.

While I creamed and jammed my scone, I said, "Alistair Grendell-Smythe and Violet came here for lunch, didn't they?"

As though I didn't know.

The ladies were as delighted to gossip as I had hoped they'd be. Florence glanced around at the three occupied tables, but there was no one we knew in the restaurant who could possibly be interested in our conversation, and besides, they were all busy with their own food and company. She dropped her voice anyway and leaned in. Mary and I both mirrored the gesture, so we must've looked like conspirators.

"I'm not one to gossip," Florence said, causing me to nearly choke on my scone, "but they looked quite cozy together."

"Cozy? How so?" When Violet had returned, she'd been annoyingly coy about her lunch date.

"Well, I sat them at the best table in the window, of course. I'd have done it even if poor Alistair hadn't just lost his father. He's such a lovely young man. And of course, Violet is quite a favorite of ours."

"That was kind of you," I said, since something seemed to be required.

"I expected them to sit across the table from each other, but as soon as they were seated, Violet got up and moved her chair closer to Alistair's."

I could see how that could be termed cozy in their Victorian view of the world. "They never seemed to run out of things to talk about, and a couple of times I heard Alistair laugh. The sound was rusty, as though he hadn't been amused in some time. She looked over at Mary—"they both had the roast beef with the mustard pickle." She glanced over at the table as though picturing the two sitting cozily in the window, sharing their identical sandwiches. "And by the time they moved on to dessert—once more, they both chose the same thing, the Bakewell Tart—they were holding hands."

I didn't know what to say about the holding hands thing. I didn't think it was particularly scandalous behavior, but I had to admit I was worried that things might be moving too rapidly. Alistair had only just lost his father under horrifying circumstances, and only a year after his mother had died. In fact, I suspected even his choice of dessert reflected his grief. "His mother used to make Bakewell Tart, you know. She used to make it for Charlie when he went there for dinner."

Mary clucked her tongue. "Oh, yes, Charlie does love a good Bakewell Tart. He's also very partial to mine, you know."

I had to bite back my smile. I suspected she was feeling a little defensive having a French Cordon Bleu-trained chef in her kitchen, so both Florence and I hastened to bolster her up, complimenting her on the excellence of her Bakewell Tart.

I had come here with sleuthing in mind, but the way the conversation had turned, I began to feel a little worried about Violet. While it was kind of her to spend time with Alistair, and they clearly liked each other, I hoped she wasn't setting herself up for heartbreak. I didn't know Alistair that well, but whatever he was normally like, he wasn't himself right now and wouldn't be for some time. I suspected any decent counselor would tell him not to get involved in a relationship right now. Even more important to me, a good counselor would tell Violet the same. He was a lovely guy, but he wasn't a good bet for her at this time.

She'd looked so happy when she'd come back from lunch that I suspected she might be reading more into the lunch than Alistair meant her to. Perhaps it was the specter of Sophie Wynter haunting me, but I didn't want Violet to end up in hopeless infatuation with someone who was currently unavailable.

I suspected Florence Watt was thinking along the same lines, for she looked troubled. "When I cleared away their dessert things, I couldn't help but overhear Alistair invite Violet to dinner in a restaurant."

"Well, that sounds friendly."

She dropped her voice even more. "Violet laughed and said he was probably sick of restaurant food. She invited him to dinner at her cottage."

This was indeed startling news, but for reasons the two

old ladies couldn't possibly know. Violet was no more of a cook than I was. If she was inviting Alistair to her cottage, I suspected—no, dreaded—that she might attempt to use witchcraft to enthrall him. It was a bad idea on every level. But how was I to talk sense into her?

Violet's romantic past hadn't been any more successful than mine. In fact, possibly less so. I knew she wanted a partner; I just hoped she'd do the usual, swipe left or swipe right, not a pinch of this and a pinch of that snuck into an unsuspecting man's food or drink.

I'd think about that later, for now, I wanted to know more about the young men who used to come here for breakfast.

I said, "Did Alistair talk about his father's death at all?"

They looked somewhat startled at my change of subject. Florence poured more tea. "As you know, I never eavesdrop on our customers' conversations. That's as bad as gossiping."

I assured her with a straight face that I completely understood.

"However, I did happen to hear Alistair say that the coroner is going to open an inquest into the death of his father." This wasn't a surprise to me. I knew through my unofficial sources that the postmortem had been completed. Death had, indeed, been caused by the massive beam falling onto Rupert Grendell-Smythe. The good news, if it could be called that, was that death had been instantaneous. The bad news was that Rafe had been right. The beam had been tampered with.

Rupert Grendell-Smythe had been murdered.

"The poor young man sounded so upset, and who can blame him? He said to Violet, 'Who would want to hurt such a nice old man who'd always been so kind to everyone?'"

I nodded. It seemed almost inconceivable to me that Alistair's father had been the intended victim.

I knew from my experience with my grandmother that losing someone you loved to murder was a terrible burden to bear. Even though Gran was still in my life, she was a vampire now. It simply wasn't the same. However, it was much worse for Alistair, as his father was truly gone. I was determined at least to get him the satisfaction of knowing the why behind such an evil action. The way British law worked, both the defendant to the charge of murder and the victim's family had the right to subsequent further postmortem. It could be weeks or even months before Alistair could finally bury his father. Anything I could do to speed up that process, I would do.

Mary also knew the pain of losing someone she loved to murder. She was obviously thinking along the same lines I was. "It will be so much better for poor Alistair once he knows, then he can finally bury his poor dad and put him to rest beside his mother."

Florence nodded. "At least he's got the weekend to look forward to."

We both glanced up at her. She looked somewhat embarrassed as she admitted that she had also overheard Alistair talking to Violet about plans for the weekend. "He said that Boris and Giles wanted to take him climbing, to take his mind off things." She shook her head, smiling a little. "Alistair is horribly afraid of heights. It was a joke even when the boys were at school. He told Violet that their plan is to frighten him so much that it gives him a break from his grief."

"Well, that's one way." I got the feeling that even though

they were supposedly all grown up, when the former students got together, they regressed.

"And how are poor Charlie and Alice doing?" Mary asked me. "We haven't seen them since the wedding. Such a terrible way to begin married life."

"I know. In a way it would've been better for them if they had gone on that honeymoon, but I think they're both too decent to even contemplate having a good time while poor Alistair is in such a state. Besides, they wanted to be here in case the police had further questions for them."

Florence looked surprised. "The murder was nothing to do with them, surely?"

"I don't think so either, but it did happen at their wedding." An older couple came in at that moment. They were probably in their fifties and had that careworn look of people who have just come from a funeral or have been visiting someone they love in the hospital. Sort of stunned and disbelieving. Mary immediately got to her feet and went forward, welcoming them. It was clear that she knew them, and since I had never seen them before, I had to assume that neither of them cared for knitting.

Mary immediately led them to the nicest table by the window, so I knew that they were special clients.

Florence leaned close to me. "It's so sad. You know I never gossip, but that couple all but lost their son to drugs. Everyone talks about the opioid crisis, you see it on the news, but it doesn't really hit home until you see the pain it causes."

I nodded and mumbled something sympathetic.

She shook her head. "And it happens in the nicest families."

I felt like smacking myself upside the head. "You're so right. It does."

She nodded. "We even knew the son. Lovely boy. Polite and well-dressed and very good in school. And then he fell into the drugs. He's nearly died twice, and the money they spent on rehab... Still, he's their son, and they'd do anything for him."

"Florence, do you know London very well?"

"Not terribly well, but I've spent time there over the years. Why do you ask?"

It was quite the change in subject. "I'm just wondering if you know Harlesden."

Her eyebrows rose at that. "Not well, no. It's in the northwest. Near Wembley."

"Near Wembley? You're certain?"

"Yes."

I wanted to bolt up there and then and follow an idea I'd suddenly had. Luckily, a group of six people arrived at the door, all speaking Italian. Since Mary was still busy with that careworn couple, Florence began to rise, making her apologies, and telling me she'd be back in a minute.

"I can see you're getting busy. And I should get back to the shop. I'll head out now. But thank you so much."

"It's always a pleasure to see you, Lucy." And then she went forward to greet her newest customers.

I had a trip to make. To Moreton-under-Wychwood.

CHAPTER 16

*W*hen I got back to Cardinal Woolsey's, Violet was humming. She didn't hum entirely in tune, but I was still fairly certain that was a love song. She was busily typing on the computer, but I doubted very much she was doing anything useful like checking the online orders. Sure enough, when I looked over her shoulder, she was Googling dinner recipes.

"Are you planning a dinner party? Am I invited?"

She glanced up at me, looking altogether too pleased with herself. "I'm having a very small dinner party. I've invited Alistair."

I put my handbag away and went to open a new box of supplies that she'd conveniently ignored while conducting her personal business in my shop. I made a noisy production of cutting through the packing tape and getting the box open before I said, "That sounds pretty intimate for a first date."

"Don't be so old-fashioned. He's staying in some stuffy hotel, and he's dying for a home-cooked meal."

I pulled out a stack of wool and turned to look at her.

"Violet, he's just lost his father in very mysterious circumstances. Do you really think it's a good time to start a romance?"

Her happy expression faded. "You should be happy for me. I finally found a nice guy. Besides, I'm good for him. I can take his mind off his tragedy."

"You can do that as his friend. I'm worried that you're taking things too fast."

She shook her head. "You know what they say about tragedy. It brings people closer."

"I also know that it makes them do crazy things. Alistair isn't himself right now."

"What are you saying? That he'd never be interested in me under normal circumstances?" Now she sounded offended.

It wasn't what I'd intended at all. "No. Any man would be lucky to have you. I'm saying that you should take things slowly. Be there as his friend and see if it turns into a romance. Don't give away your heart too quickly."

She made a big performance out of leaving the recipe website. "It's only dinner."

And she very ostentatiously grabbed a duster and began to dust the shelves, doing her best to knock a cloud of dust into my face.

Some people really didn't take criticism well.

I put away the wools and gathered some packages that were ready to be mailed out. The online store was a fun and growing part of my business, and I enjoyed looking at where the packages were going. Some went no more than twenty miles outside of Oxford, and some traveled as far away as Europe, Asia and North America.

Since Violet was still in a snit with me, I was quite happy to leave her to it. "Do you mind closing up tonight? I've got these packages to mail and then a few errands to run."

"No. That's fine." I knew darn well that the minute I left, she'd be back on the internet, looking up romantic recipes. So long as she looked after any customers who dropped in, I didn't really mind.

I took the packages to the post office and then, instead of going back into the shop, walked around and got into my red car. As I headed to Moreton, I went over in my head a new theory I had. The more I thought about it, the more I believed it might be true.

When I drew up in the small parking lot behind the church, a wave of sadness washed over me. There were big signs and flagging tape across the front doors of St. John the Divine, warning people to stay out, that it wasn't safe. The little car park was filled with the trucks and cars of workers who were presumably shoring up the roof of the church. It didn't matter that the beam had been cut through. It was still full of deathwatch beetles, and without that beam, the roof was further weakened.

As I got out of the car, I could hear sounds of construction going on inside.

"Hello," a voice said. "It's Lucy, isn't it?"

I turned to find Philip Wallington just coming out of the church. His red hard hat looked a bit ludicrous with his dark suit and clerical collar. He came closer and then removed the red hat from his head.

"That's right. Lucy Swift. I see they're already working on the church."

"Had to be done. It was too dangerous and unstable to

leave it. We have no idea how we'll pay for it. The fundraising effort had barely begun, but we've got some very determined parishioners, and there's a letter-writing campaign to try and get funding from every government agency and charity we can think of."

"That's good." I thought of Emily Bloom. If the committee was made up of people like her, I suspected they'd end up with a surplus.

Philip looked at the church as though it was a mysterious place. "I came away from London, which was supposed to be dangerous, to this quiet hamlet where I expected peace. Instead, I watched a man killed in front of my eyes."

"I know. It was awful."

"Yes. Of course, you were there too." He came closer to where I was still standing beside my car. "Did you come to see me? If you want to talk about what happened, I've always got time. It does help."

"That's very kind of you, but I didn't come here for spiritual guidance." He looked at me, a slightly inquiring expression on his pleasant face. A lock of his brown hair had pulled up when he'd taken off the hardhat, making him look more like an unruly schoolboy than a vicar.

"I've been thinking about that terrible day."

"So have I. I can't get it out of my mind."

"I keep wondering if there could be any connection between your work in London and what happened here."

He didn't say anything, but his bland expression sharpened.

So did mine. "You recognized someone in the congregation, didn't you? Someone you knew in London when you were ministering to drug addicts."

He shook his head before I'd even finished speaking, and the wayward tuft of hair waggled like a duck's tail. "Lucy, you have no right to ask me questions like that. Those programs are conducted under the strictest secrecy. Lives can be ruined if the identities of those working to get better leak out. Addicts look like you and me on the surface. They can hide their problems for years and no one knows. Sometimes not even their families. It's up to them if they want to talk about their challenges. I cannot betray a confidence."

I understood his scruples, but I had to get past them. "Lives *were* ruined. Rupert Grendell-Smythe lost his."

"I'm sorry, Lucy. I know you mean well. But I cannot betray the people who have come to me expecting that I will keep their confidences."

I realized it was a very different experience trying to get information out of the vicar than it had been getting equally pertinent information out of Florence and Mary Watt. "I'm only trying to help, just like you. I'm not officially with any kind of law enforcement, of course, but if you ask around, you'll find I do have some history of helping solve crimes in this area."

He said, "I want to help you, but my hands are tied."

Still, he didn't walk away from me. I felt that he truly wanted to help me, but he was bound by whatever oaths he'd taken or promises he'd made to those he helped, and he clearly took them seriously.

I had an idea. "I'm going to say a name. You don't have to tell me anything at all. If that person came to your meetings in London, put the hardhat back on your head. If they didn't, just keep that hardhat in your hand."

He looked at me as though that was the stupidest request anyone had ever made of him. Still, he didn't say a word.

I looked at him. Very slowly and clearly I enunciated a name. "Boris Wynter."

His eyes remained steady on mine. Neither of us moved. There was a clatter from inside the church. One of the metal pieces of scaffolding must've fallen to the old stone floor. Slowly he took the hardhat and put it back on his head. "If you'll excuse me, I should be getting back."

And then he turned and walked back toward the construction zone.

I was so pleased with myself that I texted Rafe and asked him to meet me at his place.

"As it happens, I'm on my way there now. I'll tell William to prepare you some dinner."

Even though I'd eaten all those scones and cream and tea, I knew I'd have a second meal if William cooked it. He was always so pleased to have a human to cook for, and his food was so good, I couldn't resist it. Tomorrow, I was really going to have to start my exercise program. I had no idea what that exercise program was going to be, but I was definitely going to start. Tomorrow.

Rafe must've immediately called William, for when I pulled up in front of the manor house twenty minutes later, William opened the grand front doors.

Henri, the peacock, came waddling up. I swear that bird knew the sound of my car and that he could always count on me for a treat. I'd picked up some special pellets at a wild bird store for just such an occasion. I fed Henri his pellet and told him how handsome he was. He looked up at me from his glassy black eyes as though to say, *Of course, I'm a peacock.* Then he waddled off again.

I headed toward William just as Rafe was coming down the driveway. William's eyebrows rose. "You seem to have tamed all the men in this house, Lucy. The minute you arrive, we all come running."

I laughed, but I felt a slight blush rise.

William must have felt bad. "I'm delighted to see you. I understand I'll have the pleasure of feeding you dinner tonight."

I shook my head. "Honestly, I don't need dinner, but you know what Rafe's like."

William looked crestfallen. "You won't break my heart by refusing dinner, will you? Believe me, cooking for Rafe does not tax my abilities."

"I'm happy to step into the breach. But you can just feed me some of the leftovers from the wedding reception." Even though a lot of people had come to Rafe's after the ceremony, they hadn't stayed as long or eaten as much as they would have if they weren't there in the wake of a tragedy. There must've been a lot of food left over.

He shuddered. "There isn't a scrap left. What didn't get eaten at the reception, we donated to a homeless shelter."

That sounded like a good solution. And I didn't relish eating food that would remind me of that unfortunate day. "I'm glad it didn't get wasted."

By this time, Rafe was getting out of his car. He looked immaculate as always, in a navy blue blazer over a gray sweater and jeans.

Since I'd been so hard on Violet about rushing into romance, I wanted to be absolutely clear that I wasn't doing the same thing. When he climbed the shallow steps to join us, I said, "I'm so glad I caught you. I think I've had a break in the Rupert Grendell-Smythe murder case."

If Rafe was surprised, he didn't show it. One of his many talents was the ability to keep his emotions well hidden. "Come in and tell me all about it."

"Would you like some tea, Lucy?" William asked.

"I spent an hour at Elderflower Tea Shop. Maybe I could have some water?"

We both walked straight to his library, a much cozier space than the lounge. I immediately dropped into a comfortable upholstered chair in the corner while Rafe settled himself in a leather armchair across from me. It was so natural, I realized I already had my accustomed spot, just as he had his.

He didn't waste time asking me what I'd found out, just looked at me and waited for me to speak.

So I did. "I keep thinking that if the murderer wasn't Sophie, so in love with Charlie that she tried to get rid of her rival, then maybe there was a connection between Philip Wallington and the murder. As we've said before, why choose Alice and Charlie's wedding to cause this disaster? It had to be connected to all those people who came from London."

"Including Rupert Grendell-Smythe?"

I waved that away. "Today the Miss Watts were telling me about this nice couple who are their customers. The son is a drug addict. They said, and I quote, 'It happens in the nicest families.'"

He nodded, looking grave. "That's true. It does."

"And I began to think. You remember when you said that the vicar didn't tell the police everything? He didn't tell them he'd been beaten up by people who would very much like him to stop helping addicts?"

William came in with a silver tray. On it were bottles of still and sparkling water, a silver bucket of ice, and slices of both fresh lime and lemon. If I was ever rich enough to have a butler, I was definitely going to do my best to steal William.

There were two glasses on the tray. I asked for sparkling water with lime, because I rarely had fancy water. William put three ice cubes in my glass, since he knew I liked my drinks cold. He didn't even ask Rafe, just poured him a glass of still water and added a slice of lemon. Then he said dinner would be ready in twenty minutes and quietly left the room.

I sipped my water, letting it ease my dry throat. Between the dust from the church construction in the parking lot, and me talking, I was in need of water. "What if there was someone at the wedding that day he knew from London? Someone he knew from his outreach work."

His eyes were steady on my face, but I knew I had Rafe's full attention now. "And?"

"And, I don't know London geography, but Philip's parish before this one was in Harlesden. It's near Wembley."

"Of course. That's where Charlie and his friends come from."

"And," I said with some satisfaction, "I asked Philip if he'd recognized anyone from his work with addicts."

He nodded. "And no doubt the vicar told you that he would be breaking every confidence if he shared that information with you."

"That's exactly what he said. So I said I'd give him a name and he would indicate without using any words whether he knew that person from his outreach days or not."

His brows rose slightly at that.

"So I gave him a name. Boris Wynter."

Rafe's eyes narrowed slightly. "And?"

This was the best part. So I left a pause for dramatic effect. "And he indicated that he did recognize Boris Wynter."

"Well done, Lucy."

I thought I'd done well too. The problem I was having was putting it all together. "So what do you think?"

"I think that Boris Wynter either has a drug problem, or he was there for some other reason."

"What other reason?"

"I have no idea."

"Can you find out?"

He looked slightly amused. "I thought we'd get to the part where you needed me to help you."

If I was a younger and ruder person, I would've stuck my tongue out at him. "Well, you do have a pretty amazing network."

"I'll see what I can find out."

I eyed him dubiously. "You're not acting like this is the breakthrough I think it is."

"You haven't convinced me. Where's the connection between Boris Wynter having a drug or alcohol addiction and Rupert Grendell-Smythe being killed by a falling beam?"

I stood up out of my chair. It was a habit Rafe and I shared, to pace when we were thinking deeply. I never understood quite why it helped, but sometimes it seemed as though walking up and down kind of massaged my brain. As crazy as that sounded, it helped. Anyway, as I paced back and forth, priceless books and manuscripts surrounding me, I thought about stories. The stories we tell, the stories we make up, the stories that become our lives.

Charlie and Alice's wedding first started to go wrong when Sophie Wynter had told a story at the hen party. The story of how she was meant to be with Charlie and not Alice.

When someone told a lie, we might accuse them of making up a story. Even if there was some element of truth in what Sophie had said, in that she really had seen a fortune-teller who really had told her she'd get her heart's desire and end up with Charlie, she had still bought into that story when anyone else might've thought it was a light bit of fun.

Now it seemed that Boris had dark secrets. What was his story? What I said aloud was, "Sophie and Boris Wynter both had something to gain. Sophie wanted Charlie, and maybe Boris wanted to rid himself of the man who'd seen him at a drug addiction meeting."

Rafe had been watching me, and now he too rose and began to pace. It was like two-way traffic going back and forth in the library. Rafe said, "But that beam didn't destroy the vicar. It didn't fall anywhere near him."

"No. But he didn't have to actually kill Philip Wallington. The church is now closed. Maybe the Anglican Church will decide this guy brings too much trouble on them, and they'll send him to South America. Or he'll decide he's had enough of ministering and make his own decision to leave the church." I paced some more. "Either way, if Sophie wanted Alice out of the way, dropping a beam on her head was a pretty good way to do it. Very permanent, with no need to wait for Charlie's eventual divorce. She could make him instantly a widower five seconds after he got married."

Rafe looked at me, and his mouth quirked up. "You see

her rather like Macbeth, then, being given a dubious prophecy and then deciding to rush fate by murdering everyone who stood in her way."

I wasn't sure if he was teasing me and thought it was quite possible that he was. "Macbeth isn't my favorite play. The witches are far too villainous. But yes, I suppose in a way, it is similar. It doesn't matter if the fortune-teller was just making things up; the point is that Sophie believed it and then took her own steps to make that fortune her reality."

"Even if it meant murder?"

"I know it seems like a stretch. But you weren't there at the hen party. That woman is obsessed with Charlie."

He wrinkled his nose. "I was present at the wedding, however. From where I was sitting, I could barely hear the service for all the wailing and sobbing coming from her."

"And then she left. Before the service was even over, she left the church."

"I still don't believe that she managed to cut that beam and then was able to make it drop."

"No. But maybe she pulled a Lady Macbeth."

He stopped pacing to look at me. Then he nodded, slowly. "I see what you mean. Lady Macbeth doesn't do any murdering herself. She sends others to do it for her."

"Right. With her encouragement. So maybe she got her big, strong, strapping brother to do the killing for her."

Rafe nodded. "And, at the same time, he was able to get rid of his troublesome priest."

He said the last two words as though he were quoting them. I knew he'd been alive during Shakespeare's time. No doubt they used to sit around discussing his plays. I said, "That's not from Macbeth." At least I didn't think it was.

His eyes glimmered with suppressed humor. "No. It's not Shakespeare at all. It's attributed to Henry II, who was complaining about Thomas à Beckett the Archbishop of Canterbury. Saying those words caused four knights to go out and murder Beckett."

"Stories," I said. "So many stories."

"And so often history does repeat itself." He sighed. "Believe me. I've seen it."

I wasn't completely happy with this theory, and I could tell that Rafe hadn't entirely bought into it either. "But it does link London and Moreton-under-Wychwood and Boris and Sophie."

"And it links them to Alice and Philip Wallington. Not to Rupert Grendell-Smythe."

"What do we know about Rupert?"

"Not a great deal. He was a teacher, well loved by all. His students spoke highly of him. He enjoyed a long, happy marriage, and he was close to his son. He didn't seem to have any enemies."

That was the most frustrating thing about my theory. It didn't solve the murder of the man who had actually been murdered. It solved the murder of someone who was still alive.

CHAPTER 17

I glanced at the old clock ticking away in the corner of the library, so quietly I barely noticed it. I groaned. "In three hours I have to meet Margaret Twigg for flying lessons."

He chuckled and then tried to disguise it as a cough. Not very successfully. "Flying lessons? Really? She's making you do more of them, is she?"

I turned to him. "Did you actually know that witches fly on brooms?"

"Of course I did. Doesn't everyone?"

I shook my head at him.

"Well, if you've got a big night ahead of you, we'd better get you fed." He held out his arm to show me out of the room. "Come on. Let's see what William's got for you."

How William did it, I would never know. He had barely any notice at all that he was having a guest for dinner, and yet I was treated to salmon done in a wonderful lemon and white wine sauce, with tiny potatoes, spinach and yellow squash.

I refused the offer of wine since I didn't want to drink and drive, not even on my broom.

We didn't talk about anything very much. Mostly Rafe talked and let me eat. We steered clear of any talk of the murder until William brought out a plate of fruit and cheese and biscuits for my dessert. I found my mind kept coming back to the murder, like a tongue probing a sore tooth.

"Did you find out anything more about Charlie's parents?" They'd been the other people who'd been closest to that falling beam.

Rafe shook his head. "I told you before that everyone has dark secrets. It seems I was wrong. Charlie's parents have none. They're so thoroughly decent, I suspect they'll both be sainted. The only thing that flagged me was the generosity. They lent money to people who would clearly never pay it back. Oh, and one interesting thing: They helped fund Alistair Grendell-Smythe's university education. They seem to have kept it very quiet though. I don't believe even Charlie knows."

It made sense to me that someone as lovely as Charlie had parents that nice. "Well, I hardly think they'd be targets for violence then. But why couldn't Alistair's parents pay for his schooling?"

"Not as well off, I should think. His father was a schoolteacher, and his mother had been a bookkeeper, but she gave up work when Alistair came along. She went back to work part-time when he was older, but she gave it up when she got sick."

"It's all so sad." At least I wanted to help Alistair find some kind of closure so he could move on.

I left before nine, as I still needed to get home and get my cat and my broom and I wanted to change into something thicker and warmer.

I found myself back at Margaret Twigg's cottage a little before ten. This time I didn't bother arguing with Nyx, I just opened the door and she jumped out while I retrieved the broom.

Once more, Violet and my Aunt Lavinia had come to watch my lesson. Violet seemed to have gotten over herself and was perfectly pleasant to me.

Margaret had me flying all over the Cotswolds, but I didn't mind. I found I loved flying, and it left my mind free to wander. I had a theory of the murder, but how could I test it? Sophie was in love with Charlie and wanted Alice dead. Boris was a drug addict and, having been recognized by the vicar who'd run an addicts anonymous program, decided to dispose of him. It was a great theory. All it lacked was a shred of proof.

When Saturday arrived, we closed the shop as usual at five, and I went straight upstairs. I'd turned down an invitation to go out on the town with Beatrice in favor of staying in and doing absolutely nothing.

It seemed rare these days for me to enjoy a quiet evening at home. Except that it wasn't a quiet evening at home, because the minute I wasn't actively doing something else, my mind shifted to the puzzle of Rupert's death. I was missing something, something obvious. I was certain of that. Every time I followed a promising path, it turned into a dead end. But in this maze of possibilities, one of them had to be right. One of these paths had to lead to the center of the puzzle. The truth.

I had an awful feeling that if we didn't figure it out soon, someone else was going to be hurt. Possibly die.

I fed Nyx her dinner. She only ate top-of-the-line tuna, and it looked so good—and besides, I had so little food in the house—that I opened a can for myself and made a tuna fish sandwich for my dinner.

When I opened the second can, Nyx stared at me as though she couldn't believe her eyes. "What?" I asked her. "I have not turned into a woman who eats cat food. It's you who are eating people food. So stop staring at me like that."

She looked at me with pity, which she often did, and then went back to her meal.

I took my own sandwich into the lounge and sat brooding. I found sometimes if I just stopped thinking about a problem, the answer would arrive. It was difficult to stop thinking about this because I felt so invested. I was worried about Alice and Charlie. I was worried about Alistair, and now that Alistair was connected with Violet, I had to worry about her, too. I worried about this invasion of dark witches that Margaret Twigg had warned me about. I worried that, if they invaded, I wouldn't be ready in time.

In short, I was a mess. I put on the kettle and brewed a calming tea. At least I was doing quite well in the magical tea department.

I finished my sandwich, vowing to do a proper grocery shop in the next day or two, and then sat with my tea.

Nyx hopped up on the couch and, curling up against me, began to purr. I wasn't sure if all familiars were as good as mine, but Nyx had a way of bringing my stress level down. I could feel my heart rate slow and my anxiety dissipate. Calm began to steal over me. We stayed like that for maybe half an hour, and then I sat up with a start. Nyx gave a burp of annoyance. Then she closed her eyes and put her head back down on her paws.

In the quiet, I'd realized something I should have noticed much earlier. I'd missed a clue so obvious I was embarrassed.

I tried to phone Philip Wallington, but I just got an office answering machine. No doubt he was entitled to a Saturday night free, but it didn't help me. The sense of urgency began to build in my chest.

Think, I told myself. *Think.*

I really needed to talk to the vicar, and driving twenty miles to try and track him down was not appealing. I didn't have his mobile phone number or even an email. Just the number for the church office.

I snapped my fingers as I realized I did have a way to get hold of the vicar. I called Harry Bloom, the retired detective, and asked to speak to his wife. When I was connected to Emily, I explained that I needed to talk to Philip. "It's important."

I heard her sigh. "I'm not really supposed to do this, but since it's an emergency and you seem like a sensible person, I'll give you his number." Emily Bloom was a sensible woman herself and, having been married to a detective for many years, understood that sometimes crime-solving took precedence over etiquette. I phoned Philip's mobile, and fortunately he picked up.

When I identified myself, I thought he wished he hadn't. He said, "How can I help you?" in a cool tone that really said, "I can't help you. Why don't you leave me alone?"

I understood his frustration, but I didn't have time for it. "I won't keep you long, but I need to clarify something with you. The person that you saw. Was it a drug addiction meeting?"

"Lucy, I really can't—"

"There is no time to waste. A man's life is in danger. If you won't tell me, I'll just have to go to the police, and by the time they force you to give us the information we need, another life will be lost. Do you really want that on your conscience?" Yes, I was laying it on a bit thick, but from the urgent feeling I had in my chest, I didn't think I was exaggerating very much.

There was a pause, and I thought he was debating whether to hang up or cooperate. Finally, he said, "No. Not drugs."

I nodded my head, even though he couldn't see me. "It was gambling, wasn't it?"

"Yes."

This was the part where I'd been so stupid. "Was Boris Wynter the only person in that meeting who was also at Charlie and Alice's wedding?"

"No."

I recalled now how he'd waited when we'd stood in the church parking lot, after I said Boris's name. He'd stood staring at me before he finally put that hardhat on. Now I understood he'd been waiting for more names. And I'd missed the cue.

"I'm going to give you another name. I don't have any time for games. This is a matter of life and death. Was he at the same meeting? Yes or no." I gave him the name.

"Yes," he said.

171

It was one of those times when I really hadn't wanted to be correct.

Now what?

"Lucy," he said, "be careful. There are dangerous people involved, and they won't think twice about hurting you."

CHAPTER 18

I was trying to decide what my next step should be. One thing I had discovered in my sleuthing was that knowing the truth wasn't enough. I had to be able to prove it and somehow make sure the right people were caught. But this killer had been clever.

My cell phone rang. It was Violet. Before I had a chance to say hello, she said, "What have you done?" She sounded angry.

I'd said goodbye to her at five o'clock as usual. She hadn't been mad at me then. In fact, she'd seemed in a really good mood. "I have no idea. What's going on?"

"I deliberately didn't tell you my date was tonight, because I knew you'd interfere. Here I am, all dressed up, with this beautiful dinner I had to order from a restaurant and pretend I made myself and he hasn't shown up."

That bad feeling I had in my stomach? It started to get worse. Still, I didn't want to jump to conclusions. "Who didn't show up?"

"As if you didn't know. Alistair, of course. He was

supposed to come for dinner tonight. He said he was looking forward to it." Her voice started to rise. "He would never stand me up."

"No. I'm sure you're right. Alistair wouldn't miss a date with you without a good reason."

There was a pause, and I heard her blow her nose. "Are you saying you don't know where he is?"

"No. Of course I don't."

"You didn't put a spell on him? Or detain him somehow?"

I loved my cousin Violet, and I tried to give her good advice, but I certainly wasn't about to throw magic around to thwart her love life. "No. I didn't."

In a very small voice, she said, "Then he did stand me up. Why do I always pick the wrong men?"

I shook my head. "If I knew that, maybe I could figure out why I always choose the wrong men too." I really didn't think he had stood her up, but I didn't want to tell her that until I knew more. "Have you tried calling him?"

"At least a dozen times. The calls go straight to voicemail."

"Do you have any idea what he was supposed to be doing today? Before he met you?"

She drew in a sharp breath. "Today was the day he was going climbing. With Boris and Giles. You don't think something happened to him, do you?"

"Don't panic," I said, trying to sound soothing. "I'm going into town to see if I can talk to Sophie Wynter. Hopefully her brother will have some answers."

"I'm going with you," Violet said.

That was what I wanted to avoid. "No. You stay where you are. And let me know if Alistair turns up."

"I suppose you're right, but I hate sitting here doing nothing."

"You can do something. If he went climbing and got lost, we'll have to organize a search party and find him. Get hold of Margaret Twigg. Tell her we'll need a dozen witches who are experienced fliers. Put them on standby. I'm hoping we won't need them, but let's be ready to go in case."

"All right, Lucy. I'll call Margaret immediately. That's a good idea."

I could not believe I was organizing a search party by flying broom. Either I was losing my mind or I was truly becoming an efficient witch.

I changed into jeans, boots, and a thick sweater. Nyx watched me and then, when I picked up my broom, she jumped down off the couch without even being asked and followed me downstairs out to the car.

I very much hoped I wouldn't need either the broom or the team of flying witches, but I thought it was best to be on the safe side.

Normally I would never drive the short distance from my flat to downtown Oxford because it wasn't very far and parking was a nightmare, but I felt time was running out.

I didn't phone Sophie Wynter to let her know I was coming in case she made some excuse not to see me. Better to surprise her.

By some miracle, I actually found street parking close to the hotel. Leaving Nyx and the broom in the car, I walked into the hotel and, using the lobby phone, called up to Sophie's room. I was grateful when she answered. "Boris? Is that you? What happened to you? I've been worried."

Oh, dear. "It's not Boris. It's Lucy Swift."

Her tone immediately went cold. "Lucy Swift? Where are you?"

"I'm in the hotel lobby. Can I come up? I want to talk to you."

I sensed that she was about to refuse, so I added, "It's about Boris."

She gave me their suite number, and I took the elevator up to the fourth floor.

She opened the door the minute I knocked. She was impeccably dressed as always, but her eyes looked strained, and she was as pale as one of my vampires. She didn't say a word of greeting, just held the door open and stepped out of my way so I could walk past her.

She and her brother shared a two-bedroom suite. It was elegant and spacious and, in this part of Oxford, it would be extremely pricey. She didn't bother with social niceties. "What do you know of my brother?"

I decided to answer her question with one of my own. "Why are you so worried about him?"

She looked at me as though I were an impertinent under-maid arguing with her mistress. Then, seeing her high-handed manner had no impression on me, she dropped the act. "We're meant to have dinner tonight with friends. Important people. He should've been back an hour ago. I'm worried."

I had to broach a very delicate subject, and I didn't know how to do it. On the other hand, I didn't have a lot of time for delicacy. "This is a beautiful suite."

She glanced around as though she hadn't even noticed where she was. "It's not bad. Bit small, and I miss my horses."

I nearly had to put my fingers on my eyeballs to stop the eye roll.

"It must be very expensive."

If possible, her gaze grew even colder. "Are you looking for a donation for some cause?"

"No. Frankly, I'm wondering how you afford it."

"Not by answering a lot of stupid questions. I thought you had information about my brother." She took a step toward the door, no doubt so she could show me out.

"The truth is, I think he might be in trouble."

From the fearful look in her eyes, I suspected she thought so too.

"Sophie, this is important. Is your brother a gambler?"

If I'd asked her if he juggled burning batons in the street, she couldn't have looked more surprised. "A gambler? Like one of those villains in James Bond?"

Trust her to imagine some swanky casino on the Riviera. I'd pictured smoky rooms and bookies. But I supposed gambling was gambling. "Yes."

She shrugged her thin shoulders. "He plays a bit of black-jack, I suppose, but only for fun. Sitting still so much bores him."

"Then I have to ask you again, where's the money coming from that funds hotels like this and your obviously expensive lifestyle?"

She went to the in-room fridge and got out a bottle of sparkling water. She poured herself a glass and didn't offer me one. "Not that it's any of your business, but our grandfather on Mother's side made a fortune in home baking." She raised her thin eyebrows. "Davenport biscuits?"

Even I'd heard of those, and I was from a different country. You could get Davenport biscuits in every supermarket in the UK. I'd often bought them myself.

I had the awful feeling that a theory that had seemed so solid was suddenly crumbling beneath my feet. "Where was your brother today?"

"Lucy, this is becoming tedious. If you don't have any idea where he is, perhaps you could go and find someone else to bother."

I ignored her and began to pace. Treading that plush carpet was like walking on clouds. "I'm not sure what's going on, but your brother's part of it. I think if we're going to stop him from doing something stupid, you need to tell me where he was today."

I thought she'd throw me out then, but from the way she looked at me, I thought she was worried her brother'd done something stupid as well. "They took Alistair climbing. He and Giles. I wouldn't have worried, except he should have been back by now. And when I call him, there's no answer."

So they had gone climbing. I didn't like the sound of that. I didn't like the sound of it at all.

"Do you know where they went climbing?"

Visions of a lot of broom-riding witches searching mountainsides began to fill my head. I didn't relish being one of them. Especially as I was worried we'd be too late.

I have better hearing than most mortals, and I could hear the ding of the elevator arrive. I didn't think Sophie had heard it. "Somewhere where they had to drive. That's all I know."

It wasn't much to go on, but fortunately I had sisters with some pretty acute powers. Somehow, we'd find them.

"Keep trying to get hold of him on the phone. If you hear

from him, please let me know." I turned back to her. "It's very important."

For once she didn't say something cutting. Merely nodded. "Please find him."

"I'll do my best."

Almost before I'd finished the words, I heard the whir of a key card releasing the lock, and then the door to the suite began to open.

Sophie ran toward the door. "Boris," she cried. "I've been so worried."

Boris was very much alive. He also looked filthy, sweaty, and his face and arms were covered with scratches.

He looked at me, and his eyebrows pulled together in a frown. "Lucy? What are you doing here?"

He looked at Sophie. "We weren't having dinner with Lucy, were we?"

As if.

"Of course not," she snapped. "We're dining with Lord and Lady Ashcroft, and we're late. Lucy, like me, was worried about you."

Now he looked even more puzzled. "Why would you be worried about me?"

I was absolutely over these two. I didn't have time to waste. "Boris, I need to ask you something, and it's really important that you tell me the truth."

"Can it wait? I need a shower. And a gin and tonic."

Honestly, these two and their entitlement. "No. It cannot wait. Where did you go climbing today?"

He glanced at Sophie as though waiting for her to hack me to pieces verbally, but she didn't say anything. He looked too tired to argue with me. He walked over to one of the soft armchairs. He didn't bother to take off his boots and managed to track dirt across the million-pound carpet. The chair barely dented as he dropped his weight into it. "I don't know. Giles knew the place. It was near where Charlie and Alice got married. Moreton-under-Whatsit."

"Wychwood," Sophie and I said at the same time.

"Get me a drink, will you, sis?"

For a woman who was so rude to everyone else, she almost ran to do his bidding. Brother Boris was clearly the apple of her eye. After Charlie.

Once more, Sophie opened the fridge. She reached down and pulled out a tiny bottle of gin and another of tonic. She took one look at her brother and pulled out a second gin. As she mixed the drink, she said, "Lucy was asking whether you had a gambling problem."

Even under the dirt and scratches, I could see his face go red. "Gambling problem? What kind of a stupid question is that?"

I stepped closer so I was standing right in front of him and if he stayed seated, he'd have to look up. "If you don't have a gambling problem, then why were you seen at a gambler's anonymous meeting in London?"

CHAPTER 19

*S*ophie passed him his drink, and he took a deep slurp. "I thought those meetings were supposed to be secret."

"Somebody recognized you there." I didn't tell them that it was the man who'd run the meeting, Philip Wallington. Let him think we had a mutual acquaintance who lived in London and happened to be at the same gamblers' meeting as he.

He took another drink. "I went to support a friend. And that's all I'm going to say."

"Why? Why did you go?"

He shifted in his chair, looking uncomfortable. "Because a friend asked me to. That's why. I don't know anything about gambling addictions. Didn't even know this bloke had one, but my friend told me I should go along and be supportive."

I was asking questions in the dark now. My theory had turned out to be completely wrong, and I was flailing for a new one. "How many meetings did you attend?"

He shook his head. "Just the one."

"And who was that friend?"

I didn't think he'd answer, and it was no surprise when he shook his head. "I promised. Going to those things is like going to confession. Everything's a secret. But when you listen to some of those stories... The trouble people get into, betting they'll win a fortune. And then they lose everything they have. They don't stop. They keep going back. They borrow money and lose that. Those people in that meeting, some of them had lost their jobs, their families. Some of them kill themselves. I had no idea it was such a problem."

"How did you even know your friend had a gambling problem?"

He looked a bit sullen now. "I didn't. You wouldn't. You'd never know. A mutual friend told me and asked me to turn up at the meeting. He'd been going as a support person. He couldn't make it that time. He told me to go and said to tell our friend I was there on his behalf."

Now, finally, I was beginning to see through the mist of lies and darkness to a glimmer of the truth.

"What did your gambling friend do when you gave them the message? That your mutual friend had sent you?"

He looked at me like it might be a trick question. Then he looked at Sophie, who was standing by the window sipping her water. "He didn't do anything. His hands were shaking, and he started to sweat. He looked more like an alcoholic or drug addict than a gambler. But after making me promise I'd never tell anyone, he was grateful to me, said whatever happened, I was to look after his family."

He drank again, deeply. "Put me right off gambling, I can tell you. I won't even waste a fiver on a lottery ticket anymore."

"Where are Giles and Alistair now?"

"How should I know? We stopped at the pub in Moreton-under-Whatsit and had a beer. Then I said I had to go, as I had dinner plans."

"Over an hour ago," Sophie said in a chill, clipped tone.

"Did Alistair get over his fear of heights?"

He snorted with laughter. "Not really. You can tell he wanted to though. He's a good bloke, Alistair."

I leaned in. "And you and Giles are good friends to him."

He looked uncomfortable. "Try to be."

I got up to leave. Sophie said, "Why didn't you answer your phone? Didn't you know I'd be worried?"

He downed the rest of his drink and rose. "There wasn't any mobile service on the hill where we were climbing. Then, when we got to the pub, I didn't bother calling you back. I could see the messages. I knew you'd only be cross with me, so thought I might as well wait till I got home. Now, ladies, if you'll excuse me, I need a shower. Sophie, let the Ashcrofts know I was detained. I'll be with you soon as I can."

She let out a long-suffering sigh. "We've probably lost the reservation now."

"For Lord and Lady Ashcroft? Don't be stupid."

He went into the other room and shut the door.

Before I left, I turned back to her. I'd been thinking about stories and addictions, and I thought it was time she got some home truths. "You know, at first I thought you had tried to kill Alice Robinson."

Her icy composure slipped. "I beg your pardon?"

"It was the way you acted at the hen party. And then your intense grief at Alice and Charlie's wedding. I actually believed that you had tried to kill his wife."

"That's disgusting."

"I didn't even know you, and yet I believed you'd hurt the woman Charlie loves." I put a strong emphasis on the word "loves" and watched her flinch. "Sophie, you have to let Charlie go."

I thought for a second she might cry. "But we're meant to be together. I've always known it. The fortune-teller said—"

I shook my head. "No. You have an addiction, too. You're addicted to the idea that you and Charlie will end up together. But it's not true, and it's stopping you from enjoying your life. As we heard tonight, addictions can be dangerous things. It's time to let go."

As I drove away, I had no idea if my words had pierced Sophie's fantasy world, but I hoped so.

Nyx and I drove back home. I took the broom out of the car, and as I did, I felt a burst of energy in my palm. Almost as though I'd received an electric shock. I glanced at Nyx, who was watching me with a strange look in her eyes.

Intuition is a funny thing. People talk about women's intuition, but witch's intuition? That's on a whole different level. Besides, we witches have help from our familiars and the tools of our trade. Apparently, that included this broom.

I wanted to put the strange tingling in my hand down to fatigue or overexcitement, but Nyx was still staring at me, and the word I felt inside my head was *danger*. I shook my head. I looked at the car and then the broom.

You'd think the car would be faster, but in this case, I suspected that I'd make better time and be able to take a more direct route if I went by broom. "Okay, you win. Hop on board."

I put the broom down so that the bristles touched the gravel beside where I parked my car and the broom handle pointed up to the moon. It was a crescent moon, but at least it was a clear night.

Nyx wasted no time walking daintily up the broom and sitting on it as though it were a velvet throne. I didn't find it nearly as comfortable. To me, it felt like I was sitting on a wooden broom handle.

Here we were, ready to go, and I had no idea of the direction. I tried to focus on what Nyx or the broom were trying to tell me. I knew who I wanted to save; I just didn't know where or how. Or even if it was too late.

I set a course for Moreton-under-Wychwood. Everything had happened there and I felt that that's where I would find answers.

We sailed off into the night. People often use the term "as the crow flies" when giving distances. As the broom flies might be more accurate. We flew across country, passing over Oxford, above the colleges and monuments—the round dome of the Radcliffe Observatory, the church spires, the quads of Trinity and Balliol—then out, over the river, past quiet fields, villages, sleeping cottages, and then trees. We passed over the standing stones, and they gazed up like so many pale faces, offering me strength and stability.

As we flew closer to Moreton, my plan was to go into the pub and ask if anyone had seen Alistair and Giles. With luck they might still be there. Boris hadn't left them that long ago.

I felt rather foolish. Everyone had come down from climbing safely. I didn't understand why I still felt this urgent sense of dread. The one thing I had learned was never to discount my intuition.

Or that of my cat.

Besides, I had some questions about shoes.

The church was coming into view now. I thought about Constance and her memorial. Beloved wife. I believed she slept peacefully. But maybe it was time to pay my respects and ask her advice. Visiting her on a broom seemed fitting.

I drew closer. The old stones slept silently. The bell tower was like a column of darkness. I could just make out the shape of the church, and then I gasped. I saw movement on the roof. I was certain of it. I steered us closer, and then I realized there were two figures standing on the rooftop. Was I too late?

There was nowhere to land a broom on the slate tiles, and besides, I didn't want to startle the two standing there or be seen as what I was, a broom-flying witch. They didn't seem to be struggling. They were talking.

Good.

Swiftly, I took the broom to the ground at the base of the bell tower. I dismounted, whispered to Nyx to wait for me, and crept to the door. My heart was hammering. The door handle was cold against my palm, and I turned it as quietly as I could, easing open the ancient oak door, hoping it wouldn't creak with age. It didn't.

I entered into an even blacker darkness. The stone stairs corkscrewed up inside the tower. I began to climb as quickly and quietly as I could, hanging on to the thick rope that acted as a banister. The stairs seemed endless, and I was running out of breath. I really needed to get back to that exercise program.

My feet scraped on the stone stairs as I kept climbing. My breath was heaving, and my legs felt heavier with each step.

Finally, I got to the top and had to take a minute to catch my breath. The bells were tied up, waiting to be rung again. I suspected they'd wait some time.

From the tower, there was a doorway that led onto the roof. The roof was steeply pitched with nothing but the crenelated edges between it and the ground far below. It was made of slate tiles and they didn't look very secure. There were patches of moss and I suspected the surface would be slippery.

The two men were still out there, talking. After casting a quick circle of protection around myself, which I probably botched, as I was so nervous, I climbed out of the stone arch and onto the roof and discovered that it was even more precarious than it looked. My feet slid and I grabbed the top of the tower to hang on.

I could see clearly now and even hear the conversation between Giles and Alistair. They were standing about twenty feet away from me, and I couldn't imagine how they'd got that far without sliding off the roof.

"Please don't do this," Alistair was saying. His voice was wavering, and I got the feeling this wasn't the first time he'd said those words.

Giles took a step closer to him. "It will be over in a minute. Think how much better you'll feel to have all your troubles behind you." He said it in a rousing tone, as though promising his childhood friend a treat.

"I swear there's money. Just give me a few more days," Alistair said, his voice rising.

Giles shook his head. He seemed so calm. So normal. "I can't give you any more time."

"But I did everything you asked me to. I made my will out to you. If anything happens to me, you get my life insurance."

"You made the mistake of thinking I'm stupid. I'm not. I checked your life insurance policy. You cashed it in and gambled the proceeds away, just like you gambled everything away."

Alistair licked his lips. Even from here, I could see he was trembling so violently he might fall off the roof any second. "Then what's the point of killing me? You're right." He gave a high, thin laugh. "There's nothing left."

"You'll inherit your dad's estate, since he died first."

"My dad?" Alistair took a step back and wobbled. "No. You didn't. You couldn't."

"Kill your old dad? Of course I did. And you've got no one to blame but yourself. He was as bad a waster as you, but he still had the London house."

Alistair shook his head. "No. He mortgaged it to the hilt. How do you think he paid for all those terrible bets on the horses? Where do you think I got the gambling problem from?"

"I know that. But the bank made sure he had mortgage insurance. When he died, the mortgage was paid in full." Giles chuckled. It was an awful sound. "I work in banking, remember? He came to me for help. Old family friend. Of course I helped him. Just like I helped you."

"But you know I'm good for it. You know I'll pay you back. Now I'm going to inherit Dad's house."

Giles shook his head. "No. If you got the money, you'd

burn through it in no time. I'm going to inherit your dad's house because you willed everything to me."

Alistair put his hands over his face. "You said it was security. In case I had an accident. I thought we were friends."

"Then you were a fool." He shook his head. "It's nothing personal, mate. I run a lucrative business on the side, lending money to those the bank thinks are bad risks. But when the customers don't pay back their loans, I have to cut my losses. Otherwise, people would see me as a weakling."

"Please. There must be something I can do."

A long-suffering sigh. "You can stop wasting my time. Be a man for once. Jump."

"No. I won't. You'll have to kill me. Like you killed my dad."

"Oh, very well." Giles took a step toward the terrified Alistair.

"Wait," I called out. I couldn't believe I'd spoken aloud. Now they both knew I was there. "You can't kill him and make it look like suicide. You have a witness. Me."

They both peered at me, squinting in the gloom. "Who is that?" Giles asked.

Alistair said, "I think it's Lucy Swift."

"How did you get up here?" Giles asked.

"The same way you did. And the police are right behind me."

If only that were true. If only I'd had the sense to call them. I'd been in such a rush to save Alistair, I hadn't considered I was doing a very stupid thing.

Giles cocked his head. "I don't hear any sirens. Think you're lying. Even if you're not, you'll both be dead long before they get here. And I'll be on my way back to London. Let this be a lesson to you, Lucy."

He walked forward, and he looked like a tightrope walker. All those years he'd spent climbing had really paid off. He had excellent balance, and the fact that we were thirty or forty feet off the ground on a slippery roof didn't seem to bother him at all.

He walked toward Alistair, who began to step backward toward me. And thanks for that. Alistair did not look like someone who was prepared to sacrifice himself to save anyone else. But with ever step back he teetered. He couldn't move backward as quickly as Giles could move forward. I could see that it wouldn't be long before Giles had his hands on his childhood friend.

If there were spells that would prevent Alistair from falling to his death, I didn't know them. Instead, I went with the age-old standby. I screamed, "Help!" at the top of my lungs.

The trouble with Moreton-under-Wychwood was that it was a sleepy little village, and everyone seemed to be indoors. I wasn't sure that my voice had carried very far. I certainly didn't see any lights go on or villagers come out to investigate. Undeterred, I screamed again.

"Will you stop that?" Giles said in a furious undertone.

"No. Anyway, how are you going to explain two dead bodies?"

He seemed to think about that for a second. "They say the best lies stick close to the truth. Alistair was distraught. His father dead, him in terrible debt for gambling. All hope gone. He went to you to talk about his troubles and, suspecting he planned to do himself an injury, you followed him. He climbed up on this roof to end it all, and you followed. But when you tried to prevent him from taking his own life, he took you with him." He shook his head. "Almost brings a tear to the eye." He sent us both a cold smile. "I'll be sure to send some lovely flowers to both of your funerals. And now, I really must get on."

He reached for Alistair.

I looked around for a weapon but couldn't see anything handy. There had to be something I could do. I took a tentative step forward, and another one. I put my arms out to try and steady myself, but it was treacherous up here. I slid and wobbled. Maybe I would die tonight, but Giles wasn't going to get away with murder. At the very least, they'd find my scratches on his face, his DNA under my nails.

It wasn't much, but right now it was all I had.

From the corner of my eye, I saw movement. I did a double-take and nearly fell off the roof. A small, furry and very determined face with its ears pushed back stared at me. Nyx. Riding by herself on the broom. She was coming to save me, but I deterred her. "Stop Giles."

I wasn't certain if she even knew who Giles was, but Nyx was a very intelligent cat. It was pretty obvious who was trying to push whom off the roof. I didn't know what a little cat on a broom could do, but I had great faith in my familiar.

Still, I took another step forward. If I could hold on to Alistair, at least we could make it more difficult for Giles to throw us off the roof. Giles had his hands around Alistair's shoulders now. I wondered why he didn't just punch him and then throw him off the roof, but of course, it wouldn't look like suicide if Alistair had taken a blow first. Forensics people have amazing ways of figuring that stuff out.

They were both panting now. Giles said, "Lucy, you've even done me a favor. When the police see all these footsteps up here, they'll imagine it was you struggling with Alistair, trying to prevent his death. Yes, I'm going to send some very nice flowers to your funeral."

He was so busy mocking me that he didn't see the broom coming. Nyx headed straight for his head. The handle whacked him right in the temple. He let out a cry of surprise and began to slide.

I wanted to catch a killer, not kill him. He slid down and, athlete that he was, managed to grab onto the crenellation, wrapping his arms around the old stone.

I thought he was enough of a climber that he'd either find his own way down or climb back up and try to kill us again. Either way, I didn't want to wait to find out. Nyx and the broom were several feet away, and her golden eyes were steady, watching me. I knew I could call her if I needed her, but right now I was more concerned with getting Alistair down to safety.

So was Alistair. "What a lucky thing that bird came out of nowhere," he said as we managed to climb back through the arch.

"Wasn't it?"

"I have to get away. If he finds me, he'll kill me." He went on ahead of me down the stairs, not even glancing back to see if I was all right.

"You're welcome," I said, as I pulled out my cell phone and called 999.

CHAPTER 20

When I got to the bottom of the stairs, I was in time to see Alistair run to his car in the church parking lot. He was in such a hurry to leave that he spat gravel as he drove away without a backward glance.

Now that I was on the ground and my life, and Alistair's life, were no longer in such danger, I was able to think more clearly. I knew a spell, I'd even seen it done, that would put up an invisible barrier. Since I suspected Giles would soon be on his way down the stairs, I wanted to keep him away from me.

Nyx brought the broom beside me and I felt her power as I recited the spell I had memorized from my Grimoire. And just in the nick of time, too. I heard Giles, his feet running down the stairs, much faster than Alistair or I had dared. It was a shame he was such an awful person and a murderer when he could have been such a fine athlete.

The trouble with the invisible barrier was that it was, well, invisible, and I wouldn't know if it had worked until the last second. I could run and hide, but I didn't feel like it. I wanted to stand my ground and watch Giles get his come-uppance.

He'd done his very best to kill both Alistair and me tonight, so I didn't feel too bad when he came racing toward the open door leading from the bell tower out into the churchyard. He saw me looking at him, and a very unpleasant smile came over his face.

Please work, please work, I chanted silently as he hit the bottom of the stairs and raced toward me. I nearly ran, but I was so glad I restrained myself when I had the pleasure of seeing him bang into my invisible barrier and get thrown back.

He yelled out with pain as he crashed into the wall. He put his hand to his forehead. "What the...?"

He came for me again and once more was repulsed. I could watch him do that all night, but by this time, I could hear the sirens approaching. I waited until the police cars were pulling into the parking lot. DS Barnes and DI Chisholm were first out of the car. "He's in there," I said, pointing to the bell tower. Then I released the spell, and Giles ran out, pretty much right into their waiting arms.

He turned to me, glaring. "What did you do?"

I put on my most innocent expression. "I didn't do anything. You killed Rupert Grendell-Smythe." I looked at Ian. "And he tried to kill both Alistair Grendell-Smythe and me this evening, too. Is it okay if I come in tomorrow to give my statement? You'll want to track down Alistair and get his, too."

Ian looked at me with a bemused expression. "How is it, Lucy, that Oxford CID has the manpower, resources, a world-wide network of law enforcement at our fingertips, and you got to the perp before we did?"

I wasn't sure if it was a rhetorical question, but I answered it anyway. "It was the shoes."

DS Barnes was reading Giles his rights as he arrested him.

Ian said, "Shoes?"

"Yes. At the wedding. I first noticed Rupert Grendell-Smythe's shoes were brand-new. They still had the price tags on the bottom of them. Maybe that's what made me start noticing people's shoes. And then, after the accident, of course, most of our shoes were dusty. Certainly anyone who had been near that falling beam had dust over our shoes. Even walking around the gravel car park with brand-new shoes put a layer of dust on. But Giles's shoes, when I saw him at the reception, looked freshly polished. It wasn't until tonight that I realized he got them dusty when he'd been climbing around up there in the rafters, when he caused the accident. At some point, he polished his shoes so we wouldn't notice the dust, not realizing that everyone's shoes were dusty and it was his being so clean that made them stand out."

He looked at me strangely. "That's how you cracked this case? Because of a pair of shoes?"

I shook my head. "No. It was also about addictions and the lies we tell ourselves, which I suppose is an addiction all its own. Sophie Wynter was addicted to Charlie. Rupert was addicted to betting on the horses. Everyone laughed about it and thought it was a harmless pastime. They didn't know that he was going to another town and betting all his money, then borrowing and betting more. Charlie's parents paid for Alistair's schooling. I wonder how many of his Rupert's friends helped him, not realizing they were enabling an addiction. That addiction was passed on to his son, who's also a gambler. Alistair has a problem. I hope now that he's seen the devastation it can cause that he'll get some help. Maybe Philip Wallington can give him some intensive counseling." I hoped so.

"No doubt you know where we'll find Alistair Grendell-Smythe?"

"My guess is that he's heading for his hotel where he'll pack up as fast as he can and get out of here, unless you get there before he leaves."

"Oh, we'll have him in minutes. I've already sent someone to his hotel after I got your message."

"Good. Giles admitted he killed Rupert in front of both Alistair and me."

"I'd like to give you a lift home, but—" He looked around the parking lot and clearly saw I didn't have my car with me. If he noticed an old broom leaning beside the church tower it meant nothing to him. There was a black cat sitting in the shadows watching, but there are black cats everywhere. "I've got to get to the station."

"Don't worry. I've called a friend. I'll be heading out soon."

Ian shook his head. "I have to tell you, Lucy, my job seemed a lot more straightforward before you got here." He took a few steps and then turned back, "and a lot less interesting." He said the last bit softly enough that a normal woman probably wouldn't have heard the words. Since I always pretended to be a normal woman around him, I didn't let on that I'd heard them.

~

I DIDN'T RELISH what I had to do next, which was to tell Violet that tonight's date wasn't such a great catch after all.

However, Alice and Charlie could now start their honeymoon, and, with Giles in custody, I could spend less time tracking down killers and more time practicing flying.

I was about to get back on my broom when a black car pulled into the lot and rolled to stop beside me. The driver's window slid open. "Care for a lift?"

I wasn't a bit surprised that Rafe had appeared. He had an instinct about me that was both annoying and, at times when I really needed him, comforting. "How did you know I was here?"

"Theodore drove by and called me. He said there were police and sirens at the old church in Moreton-under-Wychwood and a man being arrested. I suspected I'd find you here."

Nyx sat beside the broom, staring. "Nyx and I were going to fly back home."

"You could, of course, though I see the temperature's dropped, and William was baking something when I left that smelled like chocolate. You could come back to my house and tell me all about your evening."

I looked over at Nyx, who seemed happy to ditch the broom in favor of riding in comfort.

As we purred off into the night, Rafe turned to me. "Unless you had other plans. Then I could drop you off in Oxford."

I'd text Violet and let her know that Alistair was safe.

Tomorrow, I'd tell her everything. Now? "You had me at chocolate."

Okay, chocolate wasn't the only attraction, but he didn't need to know everything.

I hope you enjoyed Bobbles and Broomsticks. Read on for a sneak peek of Popcorn and Poltergeists, Vampire Knitting Club Book 9.

A Note from Nancy

Dear Reader,

Thank you for reading the Vampire Knitting Club series. I am so grateful for all the enthusiasm this series has received. I have plenty more stories about Lucy and her undead knitters planned for the future.

I hope you'll consider leaving a review and please tell your friends who like cozy mysteries.

Review on Amazon, Goodreads or BookBub.

Your support is the wool that helps me knit up these yarns. Turn the page for a sneak peek of *Popcorn and Poltergeists*, Book 9 of the Vampire Knitting Club.

Join my newsletter for a free prequel, *Tangles and Treasons*, the exciting tale of how the gorgeous Rafe Crosyer was turned into a vampire.

Until next time,
Happy Reading,

Nancy

POPCORN AND POLTERGEISTS

Excerpt from Chapter 1

I went upstairs to my flat. Rafe had laid the table for me and even opened a bottle of red wine. It looked both old and expensive which suggested that it was from Rafe's cellar and not the cupboard above my fridge where I kept my meager supply. He said, "William wanted you to try the meal with the wine he's planning to serve. He's very serious about his new catering business."

"I am so glad I didn't have time for a proper dinner tonight."

While we chatted, Rafe served lobster bisque. He didn't join me in any food, but he poured himself a glass of the wine and kept me company.

While I sampled the delicious soup, I asked about his work. He had an interesting job restoring and evaluating manuscripts ranging from papyrus scrolls to much more recent first editions. He said, "At the moment I'm working on evaluating the collection for a women's college here in Oxford."

I looked up at him. "For insurance purposes?"

"That's what the college is saying, but I suspect they're going to sell the collection. The college is financially strapped and word is they're about to lose one of their biggest supporters."

"Why?"

He settled back and stretched his long legs out in front of him, crossing one ankle over the other. "Two reasons. One, the most precious items in the library's collection are missing."

I gulped my soup by accident and coughed. "What?" Only since I had known Rafe had I realized how precious some of these old books and manuscripts were. "Was it stolen?"

"That's the question." He looked into his glass where the light played off the surface of the red wine as though he found it fascinating. "The collection contains a copy of Frankenstein with Mary Wollstonecraft Shelley's hand written notes."

"Wow." Even I could figure out that that was worth a pretty sum.

"There is also a first edition of Jane Eyre. Again, it's valuable in itself but also because it came with a collection of letters written by Charlotte Brontë."

"So they have research as well as monetary value."

He looked me approving. "Exactly. It's bad enough to lose a valuable manuscript, but the additional notes and letters by the authors are irreplaceable."

"Are there any clues as to what happened?"

Once more he turned his attention back to his wine. "The

principal, a woman named Georgianna Quales died. After her death the treasures were found to be missing."

"And nothing was found in her things? There were no letters? Nothing in her will?"

"It was a sudden death."

The way he said the words sudden death made me look up. There was sudden death by accident or illness and... "What happened to her?"

"Her neck was broken. She was found dead at the bottom of a stone staircase that led up to the library."

"That's a nasty trip and fall."

"It was. Worse, after a blameless tenure during which she'd done a lot to improve the college there is now a cloud of suspicion that taints her memory."

I felt there was a lot that he wasn't saying. "You knew her, didn't you?"

"I did. I would've said Georgianna was devoted to the college and to her students. There are very few women's colleges left. There were no lands except what the college sits on, so she always said that those precious manuscripts were like an insurance policy. They could be sold if needed to save the college."

"It's a funny thing. One of my knitting customers is a professor there. In Victorian literature in fact. Her name is Fiona McAdam."

He smiled slightly. "Actually that's not a coincidence. I met Professor McAdam and, since she was knitting at the time, I told her about your shop and suggested she come by."

"That was nice of you. She's been a good customer too. She was supposed to be at my knitting class tonight, but she never showed up."

"That's odd. I saw her earlier and she said she was looking forward to tonight."

Students flaked for all sorts of reasons, but I'd call Fiona tomorrow and make sure she was okay. "You mentioned two reasons why a major funder might back out. What was the second?"

"That is the more interesting reason." He glanced up at me. "A poltergeist has been reportedly causing havoc in the library."

I burst into surprised laughter. "A poltergeist? Are you kidding me?"

"Lucy, I am a vampire talking to a witch. What is so amusing about a poltergeist?"

Order your copy today! *Popcorn and Poltergeists* is Book 9 in the Vampire Knitting Club series.

ALSO BY NANCY WARREN

The best way to keep up with new releases, plus enjoy bonus content and prizes is to join Nancy's newsletter at nancywarren.net

～

Vampire Knitting Club

Tangles and Treasons - a free prequel for Nancy's newsletter subscribers

The Vampire Knitting Club - Book 1

Stitches and Witches - Book 2

Crochet and Cauldrons - Book 3

Stockings and Spells - Book 4

Purls and Potions - Book 5

Fair Isle and Fortunes - Book 6

Lace and Lies - Book 7

Bobbles and Broomsticks - Book 8

Popcorn and Poltergeists - Book 9

Six Merry Little Murders novella collection

Toni Diamond Mysteries

Toni is a successful saleswoman for Lady Bianca Cosmetics in this series of humorous cozy mysteries. Along with having an eye for beauty and a head for business, Toni's got a nose for trouble and she's never shy about following her instincts, even when they lead to murder.

Frosted Shadow - Book 1

Ultimate Concealer - Book 2

Midnight Shimmer - Book 3

A Diamond Choker For Christmas - A Toni Diamond Mysteries Novella

The Almost Wives Club

An enchanted wedding dress is a matchmaker in this series of romantic comedies where five runaway brides find out who the best men really are!

The Almost Wives Club: Kate - Book 1

Second Hand Bride - Book 2

Bridesmaid for Hire - Book 3

The Wedding Flight - Book 4

If the Dress Fits - Book 5

Take a Chance series

Meet the Chance family, a cobbled together family of eleven kids who are all grown up and finding their ways in life and love.

Kiss a Girl in the Rain - Book 1

Iris in Bloom - Book 2

Blueprint for a Kiss - Book 3

Every Rose - Book 4

Love to Go - Book 5

The Sheriff's Sweet Surrender - Book 6

The Daisy Game - Book 7

Chance Encounter - Prequel

Take a Chance Box Set - Prequel and Books 1-3

For a complete list of books, check out Nancy's website at
nancywarren.net

√

ABOUT THE AUTHOR

Nancy Warren is the USA Today Bestselling author of more than 70 novels. She's originally from Vancouver, Canada, though she tends to wander and has lived in England, Italy and California at various times. While living in Oxford she dreamed up The Vampire Knitting Club. She currently splits her time between Bath, UK, where she often pretends she's Jane Austen. Or at least a character in a Jane Austen novel, and Victoria, British Columbia where she enjoys living by the ocean. Favorite moments include being the answer to a crossword puzzle clue in Canada's National Post newspaper, being featured on the front page of the New York Times when her book Speed Dating launched Harlequin's NASCAR series, and being nominated three times for Romance Writers of America's RITA award. She has an MA in Creative Writing from Bath Spa University. She's an avid hiker, loves chocolate and most of all, loves to hear from readers! The best way to stay in touch is to sign up for Nancy's newsletter at www.nancywarren.net.

To learn more about Nancy and her books
www.nancywarren.net

CPSIA information can be obtained
at www.ICGtesting.com
Printed in the USA
LVHW081512221221
706819LV00014B/596